William Black

Macleod of Dare

Vol. III

William Black

Macleod of Dare
Vol. III

ISBN/EAN: 9783337043636

Printed in Europe, USA, Canada, Australia, Japan

Cover: Foto ©Andreas Hilbeck / pixelio.de

More available books at **www.hansebooks.com**

A Novel.

BY

WILLIAM BLACK,

AUTHOR OF "MADCAP VIOLET," "A PRINCESS OF THULE," ETC

IN THREE VOLUMES.

VOL. III.

WITH ILLUSTRATIONS.

London:

MACMILLAN AND CO.

1878.

LONDON:

R. CLAY, SONS, AND TAYLOR,

BREAD STREET HILL, E C.

CONTENTS OF VOL. III.

CHAPTER I.

CHAPTER VII.

CHAPTER VIII.

CHAPTER IX.

CHAPTER X.

CHAPTER XI.

CHAPTER XII.

CHAPTER XIII.

CHAPTER XIV.

CHAPTER XV.

LIST OF ILLUSTRATIONS

TO VOL. III.

MACLEOD OF DARE.

CHAPTER I.

HAMISH.

AND now—look! The sky is as blue as the heart of a sapphire, and the sea would be as blue too, only for the glad white of the rippling waves. And the wind is as soft as the winnowing of a sea-gull's wing; and green, green are the laughing shores of Ulva! The bride is coming. All around the coast the people are on the alert; Donald in his new finery; Hamish half frantic with excitement; the crew of the *Umpire* down at the quay; and the scarlet flag fluttering from the top of the white pole. And behold!—as the cry goes along that the steamer is in sight, what is this strange thing? She

VOL. III.   B

comes clear out from the Sound of Iona; but
who has ever seen before that long line running
from her stem to her masts and down again to
her stern ?

"Oh, Keith," Janet Macleod cried, with sudden
tears starting to her eyes, "do you know what
Captain Macallum has done for you ?   The
steamer has got all her flags out!"

Macleod flushed red.

"Well, Janet," said he, " I wrote to Captain
Macallum, and I asked him to be so good as to
pay them some little attention; but who was to
know that he would do that ? "

"And a very proper thing, too," said Major
Stewart, who was standing hard by.   "A very
pretty compliment to strangers; and you know
you have not many visitors coming to Castle
Dare."

The Major spoke in a matter-of-fact way.
Why should not the steamer show her bunting
in honour of Macleod's guests ?   But all the
same the gallant soldier, as he stood and watched
the steamer coming along, became a little bit
excited too ; and he whistled to himself, and

tapped his toe on the ground. It was a fine air he was whistling. It was all about breast-knots!

"Into the boat with you now, lads!" Macleod called out; and first of all to go down to the steps was Donald; and the silver and cairngorms on his pipes were burnished so that they shone like diamonds in the sunlight; and he wore his cap so far on one side that nobody could understand how it did not fall off. Macleod was alone in the stern. Away the shapely boat went through the blue waves.

"Put your strength into it now," said he, in the Gaelic, "and show them how the Mull lads can row!"

And then again—

"Steady now! Well rowed, boys!"

And here are all the people crowding to one side of the steamer to see the strangers off; and the captain is on the bridge; and Sandy is at the open gangway; and at the top of the iron steps —there is only one whom Macleod sees—and she is all in white and blue—and he has caught her eyes—at last, at last!

He seized the rope, and sprang up the iron ladder.

"Welcome to you, sweetheart!" said he, in a low voice, and his trembling hand grasped hers.

"How do you, Keith?" said she. "Must we go down these steps?"

He had no time to wonder over the coldness—the petulance almost—of her manner; for he had to get both father and daughter safely conducted into the stern of the boat; and their luggage had to be got in; and he had to say a word or two to the steward; and finally he had to hand down some loaves of bread to the man next him, who placed them in the bottom of the boat.

"The commissariat arrangements are primitive," said Mr. White in an undertone to his daughter; though she made no answer to his words or his smile. But indeed, even if Macleod had overheard, he would have taken no shame to himself that he had secured a supply of white bread for his guests. Those who had gone yachting with Macleod—Major Stewart, for example, or Norman Ogilvie—had soon learned not to despise their host's highly practical acquaintance with tinned meats, pickles, condensed milk, and such-like things. Who was it had proposed to erect a monument to him for his discovery of the effect of introducing a leaf of lettuce steeped in vinegar between the folds of a sandwich?

Then he jumped down into the boat again; and the great steamer steamed away; and the men struck their oars into the water.

"We will soon take you ashore now," said he, with a glad light on his face; but so excited was he that he could scarcely get the tiller-ropes right; and certainly he knew not what he was saying. And as for her—why was she so silent after the long separation? Had she no word at all for the lover who had so hungered for her coming?

And then Donald, perched high at the bow, broke away into his wild welcome of her; and there was a sound now louder than the calling of the seabirds and the rushing of the seas. And if the English lady knew that this proud and shrill

strain had been composed in honour of her,
would it not bring some colour of pleasure to
the pale face?   So thought Donald at least; and
he had his eyes fixed on her as he played as he
had never played before that day.   And if she
did not know the cunning modulations and the
clever fingering, Macleod knew them; and the
men knew them; and after they got ashore they
would say to him—

"Donald, that was a good pibroch you played
for the English lady."

But what was the English lady's thanks?
Donald had not played over sixty seconds when
she turned to Macleod and said—

"Keith, I wish you would stop him.   I have
a headache."

And so Macleod called out at once, in the lad's
native tongue.   But Donald could not believe
this thing—though he had seen the strange lady
turn to Sir Keith.   And he would have continued had not one of the men turned to him
and said—

"Donald, do you not hear?   Put down the
pipes."

For an instant the lad looked dumbfounded; then he slowly took down the pipes from his shoulder, and put them beside him; and then he turned his face to the bow so that no one should see the tears of wounded pride that had sprung to his eyes. And Donald said no word to any one till they got ashore; and he went away by himself to Castle Dare, with his head bent down, and his pipes under his arm; and when he was met at the door by Hamish, who angrily demanded why he was not down at the quay with his pipes, he only said—

"There is no need of me or my pipes any more at Dare; and it is somewhere else that I will now go with my pipes."

But meanwhile Macleod was greatly concerned to find his sweetheart so cold and distant; and it was all in vain that he pointed out to her the beauties of this summer day—that he showed her the various islands he had often talked about, and called her attention to the skarts sitting on the Erisgeir rocks, and asked her—seeing that she sometimes painted a little in water-colour—whether she noticed the peculiar, clear, intense, and luminous blue of the shadows in the great cliffs which they were approaching. Surely no day could have been more auspicious for her coming to Dare ?

"The sea did not make you ill ? " he said.

"Oh no," she answered ; and that was true enough, though it had produced in her agonising fears of becoming ill which had somewhat ruffled her temper. And besides she had a headache. And then she had a nervous fear of small boats.

"It is a very small boat to be out in the open sea," she remarked, looking at the long and shapely gig that was cleaving the summer waves.

"Not on a day like this surely," said he, laughing. "But we will make a good sailor of you before you leave Dare, and you will think yourself safer in a boat like this than in a big steamer. Do you know that the steamer you came in, big as it is, draws only five feet of water ? "

If he had told her that the steamer drew five tons of coal she could just as well have understood him. Indeed she was not paying much attention to him. She had an eye for the biggest of the waves that were running by the side of the long boat.

But she plucked up her spirits somewhat on getting ashore; and she made the prettiest of little curtsies to Lady Macleod; and she shook hands with Major Stewart, and gave him a charming smile; and she shook hands with Janet too, whom she regarded with a quick scrutiny. So this was the cousin that Keith Macleod was continually praising?

"Miss White has a headache, mother," Macleod said, eager to account beforehand for any possible constraint in her manner. "Shall we send for the pony?"

"Oh no," Miss White said, looking up to the bare walls of Dare. "I shall be very glad to have a short walk now. Unless you, papa, would like to ride?"

"Certainly not—certainly not," said Mr. White, who had been making a series of formal remarks to Lady Macleod about his impressions of the scenery of Scotland.

"We will get you a cup of tea," said Janet Macleod, gently, to the new-comer, "and you will lie down for a little time, and I hope the sound of the waterfall will not disturb you. It is a long way you have come; and you will be very tired, I am sure."

"Yes, it is a pretty long way," she said; but she wished this over-friendly woman would not treat her as if she were a spoiled child. And no doubt they thought, because she was English, she could not walk up to the further end of that fir-wood.

So they all set out for Castle Dare; and Macleod was now walking—as many a time he had dreamed of his walking—with his beautiful sweetheart; and there were the very ferns that he thought she would admire; and here the very point in the fir-wood where he would stop her and ask her to look out on the blue sea, with Inch Kenneth, and Ulva, and Staffa all lying in the sunlight, and the razor-fish of land—Coll and Tiree—at the horizon. But instead of being proud and glad, he was almost afraid. He was so anxious that everything should please her

that he dared scarce bid her look at anything.
He had himself superintended the mending of
the steep path; but even now the recent rains
had left some puddles. Would she not consider
the moist warm odours of this larch-wood as too
oppressive?

"What is that?" she said, suddenly.

There was a sound far below them of the
striking of oars in the water, and another
sound of one or two men monotonously
chanting a rude sort of chorus.

"They are taking the gig on to the yacht."
said he.

"But what are they singing?"

"Oh, that is *Fhir a bhata*," said he; "it is
the common boat-song. It means, *Good-bye
to you, Boatman, a hundred times, wherever
you may be going.*"

"It is very striking—very effective, to hear
singing, and not see the people," she said.
"It is the very prettiest introduction to a
scene; I wonder it is not oftener used. Do
you think they could write me down the
words and music of that song?"

"Oh, no, I think not," said he, with a nervous laugh. "But you will find something like it, no doubt, in your book."

So they passed on through the plantation; and at last they came to an open glade; and here was a deep chasm spanned by a curious old bridge of stone almost hidden by ivy; and there was a brawling stream dashing down over the rocks and flinging spray all over the briars and queen of the meadow and foxgloves on either bank.

"That is very pretty," said she: and then he was eager to tell her that this little glen was even more beautiful when the rowan-trees showed their rich clusters of scarlet berries.

"Those bushes there, you mean," said she. "The mountain-ash."

"Yes."

"Ah," she said, "I never see those scarlet berries without wishing I was a dark woman. If my hair were black, I would wear nothing else in it."

By this time they had climbed well up the

cliff; and presently they came on the open plateau on which stood Castle Dare, with its gaunt walls, and its rambling courtyards, and its stretch of damp lawn with a few fuchsia-bushes and orange-lilies that did not give a very ornamental look to the place.

"We have had heavy rains of late," he said, hastily; he hoped the house and its surroundings did not look too dismal.

And when they went inside and passed through the sombre dining-hall, with its huge fireplace, and its dark weapons, and its few portraits dimly visible in the dusk, he said—

"It is very gloomy in the day-time; but it is more cheerful at night."

And when they reached the small drawing-room he was anxious to draw her attention away from the antiquated furniture and the nondescript decoration by taking her to the window and showing her the great breadth of the summer sea, with the far islands, and the brown-sailed boat of the Gometra men coming back from Staffa. But presently in came

Janet; and would take the fair stranger away
to her room; and was as attentive to her as
if the one were a great princess, and the other a
meek serving-woman.   And by and by Macleod,
having seen his other guest provided for, went
into the library, and shut himself in, and sate
down—in a sort of stupor.   He could almost
have imagined that the whole business of the
morning was a dream; so strange did it seem
to him that Gertrude White should be living
and breathing under the same roof with
himself.

Nature herself seemed to have conspired with
Macleod to welcome and charm this fair guest.
He had often spoken to her of the sunsets
that shone over the western seas; and he had
wondered whether, during her stay in the north,
she would see some strange sight that would
remain for ever a blaze of colour in her memory.
And now on this very first evening there was
a spectacle seen from the high windows of Dare
that filled her with astonishment and caused
her to send quickly for her father, who was
burrowing among the old armour.   The sun

had just gone down. The western sky was of the colour of a soda-water bottle become glorified; and in this vast breadth of shining clear green lay one long island of cloud—a pure scarlet. Then the sky overhead and the sea far below them were both of a soft roseate purple; and Fladda and Staffa and Lunga, out at the horizon, were almost black against that flood of green light. When he asked her if she had brought her water-colours with her, she smiled. She was not likely to attempt to put anything like that down on paper.

Then they adjourned to the big hall, which was now lit up with candles; and Major Stewart had remained to dinner: and the gallant soldier, glad to have a merry evening away from his sighing wife, did his best to promote the cheerfulness of the party. Moreover, Miss White had got rid of her headache, and showed a greater brightness of face; so that both the old lady at the head of the table and her niece Janet had to confess to themselves that this English girl who was like to tear Keith Macleod away from them was very pretty, and had an

amiable look, and was soft and fine and delicate
in her manners and speech.   The charming sim-
plicity of her costume too; had anybody ever
seen a dress more beautiful with less pretence
of attracting notice ?   Her very hands: they
seemed objects fitted to be placed on a cushion
of blue velvet under a glass shade, so white and
small and perfectly formed were they.   That
was what the kindly-hearted Janet thought.
She did not ask herself how those hands would
answer if called upon to help—amid the grime
and smoke of a shepherd's hut—the shepherd's
wife to patch together a pair of homespun
trousers for the sailor-son coming back from
the sea.

"And now," said Keith Macleod to his fair
neighbour, when Hamish had put the claret and
the whisky on the table, "since your head is
well now, would you like to hear the pipes ? It
is an old custom of the house.   My mother would
think it strange to have it omitted," he added in
a lower voice.

"Oh, if it is a custom of the house," she said
coldly—for she thought it was inconsiderate of

him to risk bringing back her headache—" I have
no objection whatever."

And so he turned to Hamish and said something in the Gaelic. Hamish replied in English,
and loud enough for Miss White to hear—

" It is no pibroch there will be this night, for
Donald is away."

" Away ? "

" Ay, just that. When he wass come back
from the boat, he will say to me, 'Hamish, it is
no more of me or my pipes they want at Dare ;
and I am going away; and they can get some
one else to play the pipes.' And I wass saying
to him then, 'Donald, do not be a foolish lad ;
and if the English lady will not want the pibroch
you made for her, perhaps at another time she
will want it.' And now, Sir Keith, it is Maggie
MacFarlane ; she wass coming up from Loch-na-
Keal this afternoon, and who was it will she meet
but our Donald, and he wass saying to her, ' It is
to Tobermory now that I am going, Maggie ; and
I will try to get a ship there ; for it is no more
of me or my pipes they will want at Dare.' "

This was Hamish's story ; and the keen hawk-

like eye of him was fixed on the English lady's
face all the time he spoke in his struggling and
halting fashion.

"Confound the young rascal!" Macleod said,
with his face grown red. "I suppose I shall have
to send a messenger to Tobermory and apologise
to him for interrupting him to day." And then
he turned to Miss White. "They are like a set
of children," he said, "with their pride and
petulance."

This is all that needs be said about the manner
of Miss White's coming to Dare, besides these
two circumstances. First of all, whether it was
that Macleod was too flurried, and Janet too busy,
and Lady Macleod too indifferent to attend to
such trifles, the fact remains that no one, on Miss
White's entering the house, had thought of pre-
senting her with a piece of white heather, which,
as every one knows, gives good health and good
fortune and a long life to your friend. Again,
Hamish seemed to have acquired a serious pre-
judice against her from the very outset. That
night, when Castle Dare was asleep, and the old
dame Christina and her husband were seated by

themselves in the servants' room, and Hamish was having his last pipe, and both were talking over the great events of the day, Christina said, in her native tongue,—

"And what do you think now of the English lady, Hamish?"

Hamish answered with an old and sinister saying:

"*A fool would he be that would burn his harp to warm her.*"

CHAPTER II.

THE GRAVE OF MACLEOD OF MACLEOD.

THE monotonous sound of the waterfall, so far from disturbing the new guest of Castle Dare, only soothed her to rest; and after the various fatigues—if not the emotions—of the day, she slept well. But in the very midst of the night she was startled by some loud commotion that seemed to prevail both within and without the house; and when she was fully awakened it appeared to her that the whole earth was being shaken to pieces in the storm. The wind howled in the chimneys; the rain dashed on the window-panes with a rattle as of musketry; far below she could hear the awful booming of the Atlantic breakers. The gusts that drove against the high house seemed ready to tear it from its foothold of rock and whirl it inland; or was it the sea itself that was rising in its thunderous power to sweep away this bauble from the face of the mighty cliffs? And then the wild and desolate morning that followed! Through the bewilderment of the running water on the panes she looked abroad on the tempest-riven sea—a slate-coloured waste of hurrying waves with wind-swept streaks of foam on them; and on the louring and ever-changing clouds. The fuchsia-bushes on the lawn tossed and bent before the wind; the few orange-lilies, wet as they were, burned like fire in this world of cold greens and greys. And then as she stood and gazed, she made out the only sign of life that was visible. There was a cornfield below the larch-plantation; and though the corn was all laid flat by the wet and the wind, a cow and her calf that had strayed into the field seemed to have no difficulty in finding a rich moist breakfast. Then a small girl appeared, vainly trying with one hand to keep her kerchief on her head, while with the other she threw stones at the marauders. By and by even these disappeared; and there was nothing visible outside but that hurrying and

desolate sea, and the wet, bedraggled, comfortless
shore.   She turned away with a shudder.

All that day Keith Macleod was in despair.
As for himself, he would have had sufficient
joy in the mere consciousness of the presence of
this beautiful creature.   His eyes followed her
with a constant delight; whether she took up
a book, or examined the cunning spring of a
sixteenth century dagger, or turned to the
dripping panes.   He would have been content
even to sit and listen to Mr. White senten-
tiously lecturing Lady Macleod about the Re-
naissance, knowing that from time to time those
beautiful, tender eyes would meet his.   But
what would she think of it ?   Would she consider this the normal condition of life in the
Highlands—this being boxed up in an old-
fashioned room, with doors and windows firmly
closed against the wind and the wet, with a
number of people trying to keep up some sort of
social intercourse and not very well succeeding ?
She had looked at the portraits in the dining-
hall—looming darkly from their black back-
grounds, though two or three were in resplendent

uniforms; she had examined all his trophies of the chase—skins, horns, and what not—in the outer corridor; she had opened the piano, and almost started back from the discords produced by the feebly jangling old keys.

"You do not cultivate music much," she had said to Janet Macleod, with a smile.

"No," answered Janet, seriously. "We have but little use for music here—except to sing to a child now and again, and you know you do not want the piano for that."

And then the return to the cold window, with the constant rain and the beating of the white surge on the black rocks. The imprisonment to him became torture—became maddening. What if he were suddenly to murder this old man and stop for ever his insufferable prosing about Berna da Siena and Andrea Mantegna? It seemed so strange to hear him talk of the unearthly calm of Raphael's " St. Michael "— of the beautiful, still landscape of it, and the mysterious joy on the face of the angel—and to listen at the same moment to the wild roar of the Atlantic around the rocks of Mull. If

Macleod had been alone with the talker, he
might have gone to sleep. It was like the
tolling of a bell. "The artist passes away, but
he leaves his soul behind . . . we can judge by
his work of the joy he must have experienced in
creation, of the splendid dreams that have visited
him, of the triumph of completion. . . . Life
without an object—a pursuit demanding the
sacrifice of our constant care—what is it? The
existence of a pig is nobler—a pig is of some
use. . . . We are independent of weather in a
great city; we do not need to care for the
seasons; you take a hansom and drive to the
National Gallery, and there all at once you find
yourself in the soft Italian climate, with the
most beautiful women and great heroes of
chivalry all around you, and with those quaint
and loving presentations of sacred stories that
tell of a time when Art was proud to be
the meek handmaid of Religion. My dear
Lady Macleod, there is a 'Holy Family' of
Giotto's——"

So it went on; and Macleod grew sick at
heart to think of the impression that this func-

real day must have had on the mind of the Fair
Stranger. But as they sate at dinner that
evening, Hamish came in and said a few words
to his master. Instantly Macleod's face lighted
up; and quite a new animation came into his
manner.

"Do you know what Hamish says?" he cried,
—"that the night is quite fine! And Hamish
has heard our talking of seeing the cathedral of
Iona by moonlight; and he says the moon will
be up by ten. And what do you say to running
over now? You know we cannot take you in
the yacht; for there is no good anchorage at
Iona; but we can take you in a very good and
safe boat; and it will be an adventure to go
out in the night-time."

It was an adventure that neither Mr. White
nor his daughter seemed too eager to undertake;
but the urgent vehemence of the young man—
who had discovered that it was now a fine and
clear starlight night—soon overcame their doubts;
and there was a general hurry of preparation.
The desolation of the day, he eagerly thought,
would be forgotten in the romance of this night

excursion. And surely she would be charmed by
the beauty of the starlit sky, and the loneliness
of the voyage, and their wandering over the
ruins in the solemn moonlight?

Thick boots and waterproofs: these were
his peremptory instructions. And then he
led the way down the slippery path; and he
had a tight hold of her arm; and if he
talked to her in a low voice so that none
should overhear—it is the way of lovers
under the silence of the stars. They reached
the pier, and the wet stone steps; and here,
despite the stars, it was so dark that perforce
she had to permit him to lift her off the
lowest step and place her in security in what
seemed to her a great hole of some kind or
other. She knew, however, that she was in
a boat; for there was a swaying hither and
thither even in this sheltered corner. She
saw other figures arrive—black between her
and the sky—and she heard her father's voice
above. Then he, too, got into the boat; the
two men forward hauled up the huge lugsail; and presently there was a rippling line

of sparkling white stars on each side of the boat, burning for a second or two on the surface of the black water.

"I don't know who is responsible for this madness," Mr. White said—and the voice from inside the great waterproof coat sounded as if it meant to be jocular—"but really, Gerty, to be on the open Atlantic, in the middle of the night, in an open boat——"

"My dear sir," Macleod said, laughing, "you are as safe as if you were in bed. But I am responsible in the meantime, for I have the tiller. Oh, we shall be over in plenty of time to be clear of the banks."

"What did you say?"

"Well," Macleod admitted, "there are some banks, you know, in the Sound of Iona; and on a dark night they are a little awkward when the tide is low—but I am not going to frighten you——"

"I hope we shall have nothing much worse than this," said Mr. White, seriously.

For indeed the sea, after the squally morning, was running pretty high; and occasionally a cloud of spray came rattling over the bows, causing Macleod's guests to pull their waterproofs still more tightly round their necks. But what mattered the creaking of the cordage, and the plunging of the boat, and the rushing of the seas, so long as that beautiful clear sky shone overhead?

"Gertrude," said he, in a low voice, "do you see the phosphorus-stars on the waves? I never saw them burn more brightly."

"They are very beautiful," said she. "When do we get to land, Keith?"

"Oh, pretty soon," said he. "You are not anxious to get to land?"

"It is stormier than I expected."

"Oh, this is nothing," said he. "I thought you would enjoy it."

However, that summer night's sail was like to prove a tougher business than even Macleod had bargained for. They had been out scarcely twenty minutes when Miss White heard the man at the bow call out something, which she could not understand, to his master. She saw Macleod crane his neck forward, as if

looking ahead; and she herself, looking in
that direction, could perceive that from the
horizon almost to the zenith the stars had
become invisible.

"It may be a little bit squally," he said to
her, "but we shall soon be under the lee, of
Iona. Perhaps you had better hold on to
something."

The advice was not ill-timed; for almost
as he spoke the first gust of the squall struck
the boat, and there was a sound as if everything had been torn asunder and sent overboard. Then, as she righted just in time to
meet the crash of the next wave, it seemed
as though the world had grown perfectly black
around them. The terrified woman seated
there could no longer make out Macleod's
figure; it was impossible to speak amid this
roar; it almost seemed to her that she was
alone with those howling winds and heaving
waves—at night on the open sea. The wind
rose, and the sea too; she heard the men
call out and Macleod answer; and all the
time the boat was creaking and groaning as

she was flung high on the mighty waves only
to go staggering down into the awful troughs
beyond.

"Oh, Keith!" she cried—and involuntarily
she seized his arm, " are we in danger?"

He could not hear what she said; but he
understood the mute appeal. Quickly disen-
gaging his arm—for it was the arm that was
working the tiller—he called to her—

"We are all right. If you are afraid, get
to the bottom of the boat!"

But unhappily she did not hear this; for
as he called to her, a heavy sea struck the
bows, sprung high in the air, and then fell
over them in a deluge which nearly choked
her. She understood, though, his throwing
away her hand. It was the triumph of brute
selfishness in the moment of danger. They
were drowning; and he would not let her
come near him! And so she shrieked aloud
for her father.

Hearing those shrieks Macleod called to
one of the two men, who came stumbling
along in the dark and got hold of the tiller.

There was a slight lull in the storm; and he caught her two hands and held her.

"Gertrude, what is the matter? You are perfectly safe; and so is your father. For Heaven's sake keep still: if you get up you will be knocked overboard!"

"Where is papa?" she cried.

"I am here—I am all right, Gerty!" was the answer—which came from the bottom of the boat, into which Mr. White had very prudently slipped.

And then as they got under the lee of the island they found themselves in smoother water, though from time to time squalls came over that threatened to flatten the great lugsail right on to the waves.

"Come now, Gertrude," said Macleod, "we shall be ashore in a few minutes; and you are not frightened of a squall?"

He had his arm round her; and he held her tight; but she did not answer. At last she saw a light—a small, glimmering orange thing that quivered apparently a hundred miles off.

"See!" he said. "We are close by. And it may clear up to-night after all."

Then he shouted to one of the men :

"Duncan, we will not try the quay to-night : we will go into the Martyr's Bay."

"Ay, ay, sir!"

It was about a quarter of an hour afterwards that—almost benumbed with fear—she discovered that the boat was in smooth water; and then there was a loud clatter of the sail coming down; and she heard the two sailors calling to each other, and one of them seemed to have got overboard. There was absolutely nothing visible—not even a distant light; but it was raining heavily. Then she knew that Macleod had moved away from her; and she thought she heard a splash in the water; and then a voice beside her said—

"Gertrude, will you get up? You must let me carry you ashore."

And she found herself in his arms—carried as lightly as though she had been a young lamb or a fawn from the hills; but she knew from the slow way of his walking that he was going through the sea. Then he set her on the shore.

"Take my hand," said he.

"But where is papa?"

"Just behind us," said he, "on Duncan's shoulders. Duncan will bring him along. Come, darling!"

"But where are we going?"

"There is a little inn near the cathedral. And perhaps it will clear up to-night: and we will have a fine sail back again to Dare."

She shuddered. Not for ten thousand worlds would she pass through once more that seething pit of howling sounds and raging seas.

He held her arm firmly; and she stumbled along through the darkness, not knowing whether she was walking through seaweed, or pools of water, or wet corn. And at last they came to a door; and the door was opened; and there was a blaze of orange light; and they entered — all dripping and unrecognisable—the warm, snug little place,

to the astonishment of a handsome young
lady who proved to be their hostess.

"Dear me, Sir Keith," said she at length,
"is it you indeed! And you will not be
going back to Dare to-night."

In fact, when Mr. White arrived, it was
soon made evident that going back to Dare
that night was out of the question; for
somehow or other the old gentleman, despite
his waterproofs, had managed to get soaked
through; and he was determined to go to
bed at once, so as to have his clothes dried.
And so the hospitalities of the little inn were
requisitioned to the utmost; and as there
was no whisky to be had, they had to
content themselves with hot tea; and then
they all retired to rest for the night, convinced that the moonlight visitation of the
ruins had to be postponed.

But next day—such are the rapid changes
in the Highlands—broke blue and fair and
shining; and Miss Gertrude White was
amazed to find that the awful Sound she
had come along on the previous night was

now brilliant in the most beautiful colours—
for the tide was low, and the yellow sand-banks
were shining through the blue waters of the
sea.   And would she not, seeing that the
boat was lying down at the quay now, sail
round the island, and see the splendid sight
of the Atlantic breaking on the wild coast on
the western side?   She hesitated; and then,
when it was suggested that she might walk
across the island, she eagerly accepted that
alternative.   They set out, on this hot,
bright, beautiful day.

But where he, eager to please her and show
her the beauties of the Highlands, saw lovely
white sands, and smiling plains of verdure,
and far views of the sunny sea, she only saw
loneliness, and desolation, and a constant
threatening of death from the fierce Atlantic.
Could anything have been more beautiful—he
said to himself—than this magnificent scene
that lay all around her when they reached a
far point on the western shore?—in face of
them the wildly-rushing seas, coming thundering
on to the rocks, and springing so high into the

air that the snow-white foam showed black against the glare of the sky; the nearer islands gleaming with a touch of brown on their sunward side; the Dutchman's Cap, with its long brim and conical centre, and Lunga, also like a cap, but with a shorter brim and a high peak in front, becoming a trifle blue; then Coll and Tiree lying like a pale stripe on the horizon; while far away in the north the mountains of Rum and Skye were faint and spectral in the haze of the sunlight. Then the wild coast around them; with its splendid masses of granite; and its spare grass a brown-green in the warm sun; and its bays of silver sand; and its sea-birds whiter than the white clouds that came sailing over the blue. She recognised only the awfulness and the loneliness of that wild shore; with its suggestions of crashing storms in the night-time and the cries of drowning men dashed helplessly on the cruel rocks. She was very silent all the way back; though he told her stories of the fairies that used to inhabit those sandy and grassy plains.

And could anything have been more magical than the beauty of that evening, after the storm had altogether died away? The red sunset sank behind the dark olive-green of the hills; a pale, clear twilight took its place, and shone over those mystic ruins that were the object of many a thought and many a pilgrimage in the far past and forgotten years; and then the stars began to glimmer as the distant shores and the sea grew dark; and then, still later on, a wonderful radiance rose behind the low hills of Mull, and across the waters of the Sound came a belt of quivering light as the white moon sailed slowly up into the sky. Would they venture out now, into the silence? There was an odour of new-mown hay in the night air. Far away they could hear the murmuring of the waves around the rocks. They did not speak a word as they walked along to those solemn ruins overlooking the sea that were now a mass of mysterious shadow, except where the eastern walls and the tower were touched by the silvery light that had just come into the heavens.

And in silence they entered the still church-
yard too; and passed the graves. The build-
ings seemed to rise above them in a darkened
majesty; before them was a portal through
which a glimpse of the moonlit sky was visible.
Would they enter, then?

"I am almost afraid," she said, in a low voice
to her companion, and the hand on his arm
trembled.

But no sooner had she spoken, than there was
a sudden sound in the night that caused her
heart to jump. All over them and around
them, as it seemed, there was a wild uproar
of wings; and the clear sky above them was
darkened by a cloud of objects wheeling this
way and that until at length they swept by
overhead as if blown by a whirlwind, and
crossed the clear moonlight in a dense body.
She had quickly clung to him in her fear.

"It is only the jackdaws—there are hundreds
of them," he said to her; but even his voice
sounded strange in this hollow building.

For they had now entered by the open
doorway; and all around them were the tall

and crumbling pillars, and the arched windows, and ruined walls, here and there catching the sharp light of the moonlight, here and there showing soft and grey with a reflected light, with spaces of black shadow which led to unknown recesses. And always overhead the clear sky with its pale stars; and always, far away, the melancholy sound of the sea.

"Do you know where you are standing now?" said he, almost sadly. "You are standing on the grave of Macleod of Macleod."

She started aside with a slight exclamation.

"I do not think they bury any one in here now," said he, gently. And then he added, "Do you know that I have chosen the place for my grave? It is away out at one of the Treshnish islands; it is a bay looking to the west; there is no one living on that island. It is only a fancy of mine—to rest for ever and ever with no sound around you but the sea and the winds—no step coming near you, and no voice but the waves."

"Oh, Keith, you should not say such things: you frighten me," she said in a trembling voice.

Another voice broke in upon them, harsh and pragmatical.

"Do you know, Sir Keith," said Mr. White, briskly, "that the moonlight is clear enough to let you make out this plan? But I can't get the building to correspond. This is the chancel, I believe; but where are the cloisters?"

"I will show you," Macleod said; and he led his companion through the silent and solemn place, her father following. In the darkness they passed through an archway, and were about to step out on to a piece of grass, when suddenly Miss White uttered a wild scream of terror and sank helplessly to the ground. She had slipped from his arm, but in an instant he had caught her again and had raised her on his bended knee, and was calling to her with kindly words.

"Gertrude, Gertrude!" he said. "What is the matter? Won't you speak to me?"

And just as she was pulling herself together the innocent cause of this commotion was discovered. It was a black lamb that had come up in the most friendly manner, and had rubbed its head against her hand to attract her notice.

"Gertrude, see! it is only a lamb! It comes up to me every time I visit the ruins; look!"

And, indeed, she was mightily ashamed of herself; and pretended to be vastly interested in the ruins; and was quite charmed with the view of the Sound in the moonlight, with the low hills beyond now grown quite black; but all the same she was very silent as they walked back to the inn. And she was pale and thoughtful too, while they were having their frugal supper of bread and milk; and very soon pleading fatigue, she retired. But all the same, when Mr. White went up stairs, some time after, he had been but a short while in his room when he heard a tapping at the door. He said, "Come in," and his daughter entered. He was surprised by the unusual look of her face—a sort of piteous look, as of one ill at ease, and yet ashamed to speak.

"What is it child?" said he.

She regarded him for a second with that piteous look; and then tears slowly gathered in her eyes.

"Papa," said she, in a sort of half hysterical way, "I want you to take me away from here.

It frightens me. I don't know what it is. He was talking to me about graves——"

And here she burst out crying, and sobbed bitterly.

"Oh, nonsense, child!" her father said, "your nervous system must have been shaken last night by that storm. I have seen a strange look about your face all day. It was certainly a mistake our coming here; you are not fitted for this savage life."

She grew more composed. She sate down for a few minutes; and her father, taking out a small flask which had been filled from a bottle of brandy sent over during the day from Castle Dare, poured out a little of the spirit, added some water, and made her drink the dose as a sleeping-draught.

"Ah, well, you know, papa," said she, as she rose to leave, and she bestowed a very pretty smile on him, "it is all in the way of experience, isn't it? and an artist should experience every-thing. But there is just a little too much about graves and ghosts in these parts for me. And I suppose we shall go to-morrow to see some cave or other where two or three hundred men, women, and children were murdered!"

"I hope in going back we shall not be as near our own grave as we were last night," her father observed.

"And Keith Macleod laughs at it," she said, "and says it was unfortunate we got a wetting!"

And so she went to bed; and the sea-air had dealt well with her; and she had no dreams at all of shipwrecks, or of black familiars in moon-lit shrines. Why should her sleep be disturbed because that night she had put her foot on the grave of the chief of the Macleods?

CHAPTER III.

NEXT morning, with all this wonderful world
of sea and islands shining in the early sunlight,
Mr. White and his daughter were down by the
shore, walking along the white sands, and
chatting idly as they went. From time to time
they looked across the fair summer seas to the
distant cliffs of Bourg; and each time they
looked a certain small white speck seemed coming
nearer. That was the *Umpire;* and Keith Macleod
was on board of her. He had started at an unknown hour of the night to bring the yacht over
from her anchorage. He would not have his
beautiful Fionaghal, who had come as a stranger
to these far lands, go back to Dare in a common
open boat with stones for ballast.

"This is the loneliest place I have ever seen,"

Miss Gertrude White was saying on this the
third morning after her arrival. "It seems
scarcely in the world at all. The sea cuts you
off from everything you know; it would have
been nothing if we had come by rail."

They walked on in silence, the blue waves
beside them curling a crisp white on the smooth
sands.

"Papa," said she, at length, "I suppose if I
lived here for six months no one in England
would remember anything about me? If I were
mentioned at all, they would think I was dead.
Perhaps some day I might meet some one from
England; and I would have to say, 'Don't you
know who I am? Did you never hear of
one called Gertrude White? I was Gertrude
White.'"

"No doubt," said her father, cautiously.

"And when Mr. Lemuel's portrait of me
appears in the Academy, people would be saying,
'Who is that? *Miss Gertrude White as Juliet?*
Ah, there was an actress of that name. Or was
she an amateur? She married somebody in the
Highlands. I suppose she is dead now?'"

"It is one of the most gratifying instances, Gerty, of the position you have made," her father observed, in his slow and sententious way, "that Mr. Lemuel should be willing, after having refused to exhibit at the Academy for so many years, to make an exception in the case of your portrait."

"Well, I hope my face will not get burned by the sea-air and the sun," she said. "You know he wants two or three more sittings. And do you know, papa, I have sometimes thought of asking you to tell me honestly—not to encourage me with flattery, you know—whether my face has really that high-strung pitch of expression when I am about to drink the poison in the cell. Do I really look like Mr. Lemuel's portrait of me?"

"It is your very self, Gerty," her father said with decision. "But then Mr. Lemuel is a man of genius. Who but himself could have caught the very soul of your acting and fixed it on canvas?"

She hesitated for a moment, and then there was a flush of genuine enthusiastic pride mantling on her forehead as she said frankly—

"Well, then, I wish I could see myself!"

Mr. White said nothing. He had watched this daughter of his through the long winter months. Occasionally, when he heard her utter sentiments such as these—and when he saw her keenly sensitive to the flattery bestowed upon her by the people assembled at Mr. Lemuel's little gatherings, he had asked himself whether it was possible she could ever marry Sir Keith Macleod. But he was too wise to risk re-awakening her rebellious fits by any encouragement. In any case, he had some experience of this young lady; and what was the use of combating one of her moods at five o'clock, when at six o'clock she would be arguing in the contrary direction, and at seven convinced that the *via media* was the straight road? Moreover, if the worst came to the worst, there would be some compensation in the fact of Miss White changing her name for that of Lady Macleod.

Just as quickly she changed her mood on the present occasion. She was looking again far over the darkly-blue and ruffled seas towards the white-sailed yacht.

"He must have gone away in the dark to get that boat for us," she said, musingly. "Poor fellow, how very generous and kind he is! Sometimes—shall I make the confession, papa?—I wish he had picked out some one who could better have returned his warmth of feeling."

She called it a confession; but it was a question. And her father answered more bluntly than she had quite expected.

"I am not much of an authority on such points," said he with a dry smile; "but I should have said, Gerty, that you have not been quite so effusive towards Sir Keith Macleod as some young ladies would have been on meeting their sweetheart after a long absence."

The pale face flushed, and she answered hastily—

"But you know, papa, when you are knocked about from one boat to another, and expecting to be ill one minute, and drowned the next, you don't have your temper improved, have you? And then perhaps you have been expecting a little too much romance—and you find your Highland chieftain handing down loaves, with all

the people in the steamer staring at him. But
I really mean to make it up to him, papa, if I
could only get settled down for a day or two
and get into my own ways. Oh, dear me!—this
sun—it is too awfully dreadful. When I appear
before Mr. Lemuel again, I shall be a mulatto!"

And as they walked along the shining sands,
with the waves monotonously breaking, the
white-sailed yacht came nearer and more near;
and indeed the old *Umpire*, broad-beamed and
heavy as she was, looked quite stately and swan-
like as she came over the blue water. And they
saw the gig lowered; and the four oars keeping
rhythmical time; and presently they could make
out the browned and glad face of Macleod.

"Why did you take so much trouble?" said
she to him—and she took his hand in a very kind
way as he stepped on shore. "We could very
well have gone back in the boat."

"Oh, but I want to take you round by Loch
Tua," said he, looking with great gratitude into
those friendly eyes. "It was no trouble at all.
And will you step into the gig now?"

He took her hand and guided her along the

rocks until she reached the boat; and he assisted
her father too. Then they pushed off; and it
was with a good swing the men sent the boat
through the lapping waves. And here was
Hamish standing by the gangway to receive
them; and he was gravely respectful to the
stranger lady, as he assisted her to get up the
small wooden steps; but there was no light of
welcome in the keen grey eyes. He quickly
turned away from her to give his orders; for
Hamish was on this occasion skipper, and had
donned a smart suit of blue with brass buttons.
Perhaps he would have been prouder of his
buttons, and of himself, and of the yacht he
had sailed for so many years, if it had been
any other than Gertrude White who had now
stepped on board.

But on the other hand, Miss White was quite
charmed with this shapely vessel and all its
contents. If the frugal ways and commonplace duties and conversation of Castle Dare
had somewhat disappointed her, and had seemed
to her not quite in accordance with the heroic
traditions of the clans, here, at least, was some-

thing which she could recognise as befitting her
notion of the name and position of Sir Keith
Macleod. Surely it must be with a certain
masterful sense of possession that he would
stand on those white decks, independent of all
the world besides, with those sinewy, sun-
browned, handsome fellows ready to go anywhere with him at his bidding? It is true
that Macleod, in showing her over the yacht,
seemed to know far too much about tinned
meats; and he exhibited with some pride a
cunning device for the stowage of soda-water;
and he even went the length of explaining to
her the capacities of the linen-chest; but then
she could not fail to see that in his eagerness to
interest and amuse her, he was as garrulous as
a schoolboy showing to his companion a new
toy. Miss White sat down in the saloon;
and Macleod, who had but little experience in
attending on ladies, and knew of but one thing
that it was proper to recommend, said,—

"And will you have a cup of tea now,
Gertrude? Johnny will get it to you in a
moment."

"No, thank you," said she, with a smile ; for
she knew not how often he had offered her a
cup of tea since her arrival in the Highlands.
"But do you know, Keith, your yacht has a
terrible bachelor look about it? All the com-
forts of it are in this saloon and in those two
nice little state-rooms. Your lady's cabin looks
very empty ; it is too elegant and fine, as if you
were afraid to leave a book or a matchbox in it.
Now if you were to turn this into a lady's yacht,
you would have to remove that pipe-rack, and
the guns and rifles and bags."

"Oh," said he anxiously, "I hope you do
not smell any tobacco?"

"Not at all," said she. "It was only a
fancy. Of course you are not likely to turn
your yacht into a lady's yacht."

He started and looked at her. But she
had spoken quite thoughtlessly, and had now
turned to her father.

When they went on deck again they found
that the *Umpire*, beating up in the face of a
light northerly breeze, had run out for a long
tack almost to the Dutchman's Cap ; and

from a certain distance they could see the
grim shores of this desolate island, with its
faint tinge of green grass over the brown
of its plateau of rock. And then Hamish
called out, "Ready about!" and presently
they were slowly leaving behind that lonely
Dutchman and making away for the distant
entrance to Loch Tua. The breeze was slight;
they made but little way; far on the blue
waters they watched the white gulls sitting
buoyant; and the sun was hot on their hands.
What did they talk about in this summer
idleness? Many a time he had dreamed of
his thus sailing over the clear seas with the
fair Fionaghal from the south, until at times
his heart, grown sick with yearning, was ready
to despair of the impossible. And yet here
she was sitting on a deck-stool near him—
the wide-apart, long-lashed eyes occasionally
regarding him—a neglected book open on her
lap—the small gloved hands toying with the
cover. Yet there was no word of love spoken.
There was only a friendly conversation, and
the idle passing of a summer day. It was

something to know that her breathing was near him.

Then the breeze quite died away, and they were left altogether motionless on the glassy blue sea. The great sails hung limp, without a single flap or quiver in them ; the red ensign clung to the jigger-mast ; Hamish, though he stood by the tiller, did not even put his hand on that bold and notable representation in wood of the sea-serpent.

"Come now, Hamish," Macleod said, fearing this monotonous idleness would weary his fair guest, "you will tell us one of the old stories that you used to tell me when I was a boy."

Hamish had indeed told the young Macleod many a mysterious tale of magic and adventure, but he was not disposed to repeat any one of these in broken English in order to please this lady from the south.

"It is no more of the stories I hef now, Sir Keith," said he. "It wass a long time since I had the stories."

"Oh, I could construct one myself," said Miss

White, lightly. "Don't I know how they all begin? '*There was once a king in Erin, and he had a son; and this son it was who would take the world for his pillow. But before he set out on his travels, he took counsel of the falcon, and the hoodie, and the otter. And the falcon said to him, Go to the right; and the hoodie said to him, You will be wise now if you go to the left; but the otter said to him, Now take my advice,*' &c., &c."

"You have been a diligent student," Macleod said, laughing heartily. "And indeed you might go on with the story and finish it; for who knows now when we shall get back to Dare?"

It was after a long period of thus lying in dead calm—with the occasional appearance of a guillemot on the surface of the shining blue sea —that Macleod's sharply observant eye was attracted by an odd thing that appeared far away at the horizon.

"What do you think is that now?" said he, with a smile.

They looked steadfastly, and saw only a thin

line of silver light, almost like the back of a knife, in the distant dark blue.

"The track of a seal swimming under water," Mr. White suggested.

"Or a shoal of fish," his daughter said.

"Watch!"

The sharp line of light slowly spread; a trembling silver-grey took the place of the dark blue; it looked as if invisible fingers were rushing out and over the glassy surface. Then they felt a cool freshness in the hot air; the red ensign swayed a bit; then the great mainsail flapped idly; and finally the breeze came gently blowing over the sea, and on again they went through the now rippling water. And as the slow time passed, in the glare of the sunlight, Staffa lay on the still water a dense mass of shadow; and they went by Lunga; and they drew near to the point of Gometra, where the black skarts were sitting on the exposed rocks. It was like a dream of sunlight, and fair colours, and summer quiet.

"I cannot believe," said she to him, "that all those fierce murders and revenges took place in such beautiful scenes as these. How could they ?"

And then, in the broad and still waters of Loch Tua, with the lovely rocks of Ulva close by them, they were again becalmed; and now it was decided that they should leave the yacht there at anchor, and should get into the gig and be quietly pulled through the shallow channel between Ulva and Mull that connects Loch-Tua with Loch-na-Keal. Macleod had been greatly favoured by the day chosen at haphazard for this water promenade; at the end of it he was gladdened to hear Miss White say that she had never seen anything so lovely on the face of the earth.

And yet it was merely a question of weather. To-morrow they might come back and find the water a ruffled leaden colour; the waves washing over the rocks; Ben-More invisible behind driving clouds. But now, as those three sat in the stern of the gig, and were gently pulled along by the sweep of the oars, it seemed to one at least of them that she must have got into fairyland. The rocky

shores of Ulva lay on one side of this
broad and winding channel; the flatter shores
of Mull on the other; and between lay a
perfect mirror of water in which everything
was so accurately reflected that it was quite
impossible to define the line at which the
water and the land met. In fact, so vivid
was the reflection of the blue and white sky
on the surface of the water that it appeared
to her as if the boat were suspended in mid-air:
a sky below, a sky above. And then the beauty
of the landscape that enclosed this wonderful
mirror—the soft green foliage above the Ulva
rocks; the brillant yellow brown of the seaweed, with here and there a grey heron standing
solitary and silent as a ghost over the pools;
ahead of them, towering above this flat and
shining and beautiful landscape, the awful
majesty of the mountains around Loch-na-Keal
—the monarch of them, Ben-More, showing a
cone of dark and thunderous purple under a
long and heavy swathe of cloud. Far away,
too, on their right, stretched the splendid
rampart of the Gribun cliffs, a soft sunlight

on the grassy greens of their summits; a pale
and brilliant blue in the shadows of the huge
and yawning caves. And so still it was, and
the air so fine and sweet: it was a day for the
idling of happy lovers.

What jarred, then? Not the silent appearance of the head of a seal in that shining plain
of blue and white; for the poor old fellow
only regarded the boat for a second or two
with his large and pathetic eyes, and then
quietly disappeared. Perhaps it was this—
that Miss White was leaning over the side
of the boat, and admiring very much the
wonderful hues of groups of seaweed below,
that were all distinctly visible in the marvel-
lously clear water. There were beautiful green
plants that spread their flat fingers over the
silver-white sands; and huge rolls of purple
and sombre brown; and long strings that came
up to the surface—the traceries and decorations
of these haunts of the mermaid.

"It is like a pantomime," she said. "You
would expect to see a burst of limelight and
Neptune appearing with a silver trident and

crown. Well, it only shows that the scene-
painters are nearer nature than most people
imagine. I should never have thought there
was anything so beautiful in the sea."

And then again she said, when they had
rounded Ulva, and got a glimpse of the open
Atlantic again,

"Where is it, Keith, you proposed to sink all
the theatres in England, for the benefit of the
dolphins and the lobsters?"

He did not like these references to the
theatre.

"It was only a piece of nonsense," said he,
abruptly.

But then she begged him so prettily to get
the men to sing the boat-song for her that he
good-humouredly took out a sheet of paper
and a pencil and said to her—

"If I were to write it down for you, I must
write it as it is pronounced. For how would
you know that *Fhir a bhata, na horo eile* is
pronounced *Feer a vahta na horo ailya?*"

"And perhaps, then," said she with a charming smile, "writing it down would spoil it

altogether ? But you will ask them to sing it for me ? "

He said a word or two in the Gaelic to Duncan, who was rowing stroke; and Duncan answered with a short, quick laugh of assent.

" I have asked them if they would drink your health," Macleod said, " and they have not refused. It would be a great compliment to them if you would fill out the whisky yourself: here is my flask."

She took that formidable vessel in her small hands; and the men rested on their oars; and then the metal cup was passed along. Whether it was the dram, or whether it was the old familiar chorus they struck up—

> " *Fhir a bhata (na horo eile)*
> *Fhir a bhata (na horo eile)*
> *Fhir a bhata (na horo eile)*
> *Chead soire slann leid ge thobh a theid u,*"

certain it is that the boat swung forward with a new strength, and ere long they beheld in the distance the walls of Castle Dare. And here was Janet at the small quay, greatly distressed because of the discomfort to which Miss White must have been subjected.

"But I have just been telling Sir Keith," she said with a sweet smile, "that I have come through the most beautiful place I have ever seen in the world."

This was not, however, what she was saying to herself when she reached the privacy of her own room. Her thoughts took a different turn.

"And if it does seem impossible"—this was her inward speech to herself—"that those wild murders should have been committed in so beautiful a place, at least there will be a fair chance of one occurring when I tell him that I have signed an engagement that will last till Christmas. But what good could come of being in a hurry?"

CHAPTER IV.

A CAVE IN MULL.

OF love not a single word had so far been said between these two. It was a high sense of courtesy that on his part had driven him to exercise this severe self-restraint; he would not invite her to be his guest, and then take advantage of the various opportunities offered to plague her with the vehemence and passionate yearning of his heart. For during all those long winter months he had gradually learned, from the correspondence which he so carefully studied, that she rather disliked protestation; and when he hinted that he thought her letters to him were somewhat cold, she only answered with a playful humour; and when he tried to press her to some declaration about her leaving the stage or about the time of their marriage,

she evaded the point with an extreme cleverness
which was so good-natured and friendly that
he could scarcely complain. Occasionally there
were references in these letters that awakened
in his breast a tumult of jealous suspicions and
fears ; but then again he consoled himself by
looking forward to the time when she should
be released from all those environments that he
hated and dreaded. He would have no more
fear when he could take her hand and look into
her eyes.

And now that Miss Gertrude White was
actually in Castle Dare—now that he could
walk with her along the lonely mountain-slopes
and show her the wonders of the western seas
and the islands—what was it that still occa-
sioned that vague unrest ? His nervous anxiety
that she should be pleased with all she saw ?
Or a certain critical coldness in her glance ? Or
the consciousness that he was only entertaining
a passing visitor—a beautiful bird that had
alighted on his hand, and that the next moment
would be winging its flight away into the silvery
south ?

"You are becoming a capital sailor," he said to her one day, with a proud light on his face. "You have no fear at all of the sea now."

He and she and the cousin Janet—Mr. White had some letters to answer, and had stayed at home—were in the stern of the gig, and they were being rowed along the coast below the giant cliffs of Gribun. Certainly if Miss White had confessed to being a little nervous, she might have been excused. It was a beautiful, fresh, breezy, summer-day; but the heavy Atlantic swell that slowly raised and lowered the boat as the men rowed along, passed gently and smoothly on, and then went booming and roaring and crashing over the sharp black rocks that were quite close at hand.

"I think I would soon get over my fear of the sea," said she, gently.

Indeed it was not that that was most likely to impress her on this bright day—it was the awful loneliness and desolation of the scene around her. All along the summit of the great cliffs lay heavy banks of cloud that moved and wreathed themselves together, with mysterious patches of

darkness here and there that suggested the
entrance into far valleys in the unseen mountains behind.   And if the outer surface of these
precipitous cliffs was brightened by sunlight, and
if there was a sprinkling of grass on the ledges,
every few minutes they passed the yawning archway of a huge cavern, around which the sea was
roaring with a muffled and thunderous noise.   He
thought she would be interested in the extra-
ordinary number and variety of the sea-birds
about—the solemn cormorants sitting on the
ledges, the rock-pigeons shooting out from the
caves, the sea-pyots whirring along the rocks
like lightning-flashes of colour, the lordly osprey,
with his great wings outstretched and motionless, sailing slowly in the far blue overhead.   And
no doubt she looked at all these things with a
forced interest ; and she herself now could name
the distant islands out in the tossing Atlantic ;
and she had in a great measure got accustomed
to the amphibious life at Dare.   But as she
listened to the booming of the waves around
those awful recesses ; and as she saw the jagged
and angry rocks suddenly appear through the

liquid mass of the falling sea; and as she looked
abroad on the unknown distances of that troubled
ocean and thought of the life on those remote
and lonely islands, the spirit of a summer
holiday forsook her altogether, and she was
silent.

"And you will have no fear of the beast when
you go into Mackinnon's cave," said Janet
Macleod to her, with a friendly smile, "because
no one has ever heard of it again. Do you know,
it was a strange thing. They saw in the sand
the footprint of an animal that is not known to
any one about here; even Keith himself did not
know what it was——"

"I think it was a wild cat," said he.

"And the men had nothing to do just then;
so they went all about the caves, but they could
see nothing of it. And it has never come back
again."

"And I suppose you are not anxious for its
coming back?" Miss White said.

"Perhaps you will be very lucky and see it
some day, and I know that Keith would like to
shoot it, whatever it is."

"That is very likely," Miss White said, without any apparent sarcasm.

By and by they paused opposite the entrance to a cave that seemed even larger and blacker than the others; and then Miss White discovered that they were considering at what point they could most easily effect a landing. Already through the singularly clear water she could make out vague green masses that told of the presence of huge blocks of yellow rock far below them; and as they cautiously went further towards the shore—a man at the bow calling out to them — these blocks of rock became clearer and clearer, until it seemed as if the glassy billows that glided under the boat, and then went crashing in white foam a few yards beyond, must inevitably transfix the frail craft on one of the jagged points. But at length they managed to run the bow of the gig into a somewhat sheltered place, and two of the men, jumping knee-deep into the water, hauled the keel still further over the grating shell-fish of the rock; and then Macleod, scrambling out, assisted Miss White to land.

"Do you not come with us?" Miss White called back to the boat.

"Oh, it is many a time I have been in the cave," said Janet Macleod; "and I will have the luncheon ready for you. But you must not stay long in the cave, for it is cold and damp."

He took her hand, for the scrambling over the rough rocks and stones was dangerous work for unfamiliar ankles. They drew nearer to this awful thing, that rose far above them, and seemed waiting to enclose them and shut them in for ever. And whereas about the other caves there were plenty of birds flying, with their shrill screams denoting their terror or resentment, there was no sign of life at all about this black and yawning chasm, and there was an absolute silence but for the rolling of the breakers behind them that only produced vague and wandering echoes. As she advanced over the treacherous shingle, she became conscious of a sort of twilight appearing around her. A vast black thing — black as night and still as the grave — was ahead of her; but already the change from the blaze of sunlight outside to this partial darkness seemed strange on the eyes. The air grew colder. As she looked up at the tremendous walls, and at the mysterious blackness beyond, she grasped his hand more tightly, though the walking on the wet sand was now comparatively easy. And as they went further and further into this blackness, there was only a faint strange light that made an outline of the back of his figure, leaving his face in darkness ; and when he stooped to examine the sand, she turned and looked back, and behold, the vast portal by which they entered had now dwindled down into a small space of bewildering white.

"No," said he, and she was startled by the hollow tones of his voice, "I cannot find any traces of the beast now ; they have all gone."

Then he produced a candle, and lit it ; and as they advanced further into the blackness, there was only visible this solitary star of red fire, that threw dulled mysterious gleams from time to time on some projecting rock.

"You must give me your hand again, Keith," said she, in a low voice ; and when he shifted the

candle, and took her hand in his, he found that
it was trembling somewhat.

"Will you go any further?" said he.

"No."

They stood and looked around. The darkness
seemed without limit; the red light was in-
sufficient to produce anything like an outline of
this immense place, even in faint and wandering
gleams.

"If anything were to move, Keith," said she,
"I should die."

"Oh, nonsense," said he, in a cheerful way;
but the hollow echoes of the cavern made his
voice sound sepulchral. "There is no beast at
all in here, you may be sure. And I have often
thought of the fright a wild cat or a beaver may
have got when he came in here in the night, and
then discovered he had stumbled on a lot of
sleeping men——"

"Of men!"

"They say this was a sanctuary of the Cul-
dees; and I often wonder how the old chaps got
their food. I am afraid they must have often
fallen back on the young cormorants: that is.

what Major Stewart calls an expeditious way of
dining, for you eat two courses, fish and meat,
at the same time.   And if you go further along,
Gertrude, you will come to the great altar-stone
they used."

"I would rather not go," said she.   "I—I do
not like this place.   I think we will go back
now, Keith."

As they cautiously made their way back to the
glare of the entrance, she still held his hand
tight; and she did not speak at all.   Their foot-
steps echoed strangely in this hollow space.
And then the air grew suddenly warm; and
there was a glow of daylight around; and
although her eyes were rather bewildered, she
breathed more freely, and there was a look of
relief on her face.

"I think I will sit down for a moment, Keith,"
said she; and then he noticed, with a sudden
alarm, that her cheeks were rather pale.

"Are you ill?" said he, with a quick anxiety
in his eyes.   "Were you frightened?"

"Oh, no!" said she, with a forced cheerfulness, and she sat down for a moment on one of

the smooth boulders. "You must not think I am such a coward as that. But—the chilling atmosphere—the change—made me a little faint."

"Shall I run down to the boat for some wine for you? I know that Janet has brought some claret."

"Oh, not at all!" said she—and he saw with a great delight that her colour was returning. "I am quite well now. But I will rest for a minute, if you are in no hurry, before scrambling down those stones again."

He was in no hurry; on the contrary, he sate down beside her and took her hand.

"You know, Gerty," said he, "it will be some time before I can learn all that you like and dislike, and what you can bear, and what pleases you best; it will be some time, no doubt; but then when I have learned, you will find that no one will look after you so carefully as I will."

"I know you are very kind to me," said she, in a low voice.

"And now," said he, very gently and even

timidly, but his firm hand held her languid one with something of a more nervous clasp, "if you would only tell me, Gerty, that on such and such a day you would leave the stage altogether, and on such and such a day you would let me come to London—and you know the rest—then I would go to my mother, and there would be no need of any more secrecy; and instead of her treating you merely as a guest, she would look on you as her daughter, and you might talk with her frankly."

She did not at all withdraw the small gloved hand, with its fringe of fur at the end of the narrow sleeve. On the contrary, as it lay there in his warm grasp, it was like the small, white, furred foot of a ptarmigan, so little and soft and gentle was it.

"Well, you know, Keith," she said, with a great kindness in the clear eyes, though they were cast down, "I think the secret between you and me should be known to nobody at all but ourselves—any more than we can reasonably help. And it is a very great step to take; and you must not expect me to be in a hurry, for no good ever came of that. I did not think you would have cared so much —I mean, a man has so many distractions and occupations of shooting, and going away in your yacht, and all that—I fancy—I am a little surprised — that you make so much of it. We have a great deal to learn yet, Keith; we don't know each other very well. By and by we may be quite sure that there is no danger; that we understand each other; that nothing and nobody is likely to interfere. But wouldn't you prefer to be left in the meantime just a little bit free—not quite pledged, you know, to such a serious thing—— ? "

He had been listening to these faltering phrases in a kind of dazed and pained stupor. It was like the water overwhelming a drowning man. But at last he cried out—and he grasped both her hands in the sudden vehemence of the moment—

" Gerty, you are not drawing back ! You do not despair of our being husband and wife ! What is it that you mean ? "

" O Keith ! " said she, quickly withdrawing

one of her hands, "you frighten me when you talk like that. You do not know what you are doing—you have hurt my wrist."

"Oh, I hope not!" said he "Have I hurt your hand, Gerty?—and I would cut off one of mine to save you a scratch! But you will tell me now that you have no fears—that you don't want to draw back! I would like to take you back to Dare, and be able to say to every one, 'Do you know that this is my wife—that by and by she is coming to Dare—and you will all be kind to her for her own sake and for mine.' And if there is anything wrong, Gerty—if there is anything you would like altered, I would have it altered. We have a rude way of life; but every one would be kind to you. And if the life here is too rough for you, I would go anywhere with you that you choose to live. I was looking at the houses in Essex. I would go to Essex—or anywhere you might wish—that need not separate us at all. And why are you so cold and distant, Gerty? Has anything happened here to displease

you? Have we frightened you by too much
of the boats ₍and of the sea? Would you
rather live in an English county away from
the sea? But I would do that for you, Gerty
—if I was never to see a sea-bird again."

And in spite of himself tears rose quickly
to his eyes; for she seemed so far away from
him, even as he held her hand; and his
heart would speak at last—or break.

"It was all the winter months I was saying
to myself, 'Now you will not vex her with too
much pleading, for she has much trouble
with her work; and that is enough; and a
man can bear his own trouble.' And once
or twice, when we have been caught in a
bad sea, I said to myself, 'And what matter
now if the end comes?—for perhaps that
would only release her.' But then again,
Gerty, I thought of the time you gave me
the red rose; and I said 'Surely her heart
will not go away from me; and I have plenty
to live for yet!'"

Then she looked him frankly in the face,
with those beautiful, clear, sad eyes.

"You deserve all the love a woman can give you, Keith; for you have a man's heart. And I wish I could make you a fair return for all your courage, and gentleness, and kindness——"

"Ah, do not say that," he said, quickly. "Do not think I am complaining of you, Gerty. It is enough—it is enough—I thank God for His mercy to me; for there never was any man so glad as I was when you gave me the red rose. And now, sweetheart—now you will tell me that I will put away all this trouble and have no more fears; and there will be no need to think of what you are doing far away; and there will be one day that all the people will know—and there will be laughing and gladness that day—and if we will keep the pipes away from you, all the people about will have the pipes, and there will be a dance and a song that day. Ah, Gerty, you must not think harshly of the people about here. They have their ways. They would like to please you. But my heart is with them; and a marriage-day

would be no marriage-day to me that I
did not spend among my own people—my
own people."

He was talking quite wildly. She had
seen him in this mood once or twice before;
and she was afraid.

"But you know, Keith," said she, gently, and
with averted eyes, "a great deal has to be done
before then. And a woman is not so impulsive
as a man; and you must not be angry if I beg
for a little time——"

"And what is time?" said he, in the same
glad and wild way—and now it was his hand
holding hers that was trembling. "It will all
go by in a moment—like a dream—when we
know that the one splendid day is coming. And
I will send a haunch to the Dubh-Artach men
that morning; and I will send a haunch to
Skerryvore; and there will not be a man in
Iona, or Coll, or Ulva, that will not have his
dram that day. And what will you do, Gerty—
what will you do? Oh, I will tell you now
what you will do on that morning. You will
take out some sheets of the beautiful, small,

scented paper; and you will write to this
theatre and to that theatre : ' *Good-bye—perhaps
you were useful to me once, and I bear you
no ill-will : but—Good-bye for ever and ever !* '
And I will have all the children that I took
to the Crystal Palace last summer given a
fine dinner; and the six boy-pipers will play
Mrs. Macleod of Raasay again ; and they
will have a fine reel once more. There will be
many a one know that you are married that
day, Gerty. And when is the day to be, Gerty?
Cannot you tell me now?"

"There is a drop of rain!" she exclaimed ;
and she suddenly sprang to her feet. The skies
were black overhead. "Oh, dear me," she said,
"how thoughtless of us to leave your poor cousin
Janet in that open boat, and a shower coming
on! Please give me your hand now, Keith.
And you must not take all these things so
seriously to heart, you know; or I will say you
have not the courage of a feeble woman like
myself. Do you think the shower will pass
over?"

"I do not know," said he, in a vague way

as if he had not quite understood the question ; but he took her hand, and in silence guided her down to the rocks, where the boat was ready to receive them.

And now they saw the strange transformation that had come over the world. The great troubled sea was all of a dark slate-green, with no glad ripples of white, but with long squally drifts of black ; and a cold wind was blowing gustily in ; and there were hurrying clouds of a leaden hue tearing across the sky. As for the islands—where were they ? Ulva was visible, to be sure, and Colonsay : both of them a heavy and gloomy purple ; and nearer at hand the rock of Erisgeir showed in a wan grey light between the louring sky and the squally sea ; but Lunga, and Fladda, and Staffa, and Iona, and even the long promontory of the Ross of Mull, were all hidden away behind the driving mists of rain.

"O you lazy people!" Janet Macleod cried cheerfully—she was not at all frightened by the sudden storm. "I thought the wild beast had killed you in the cave. And shall we have luncheon now, Keith, or go back at once ? "

He cast an eye towards the westward horizon, and the threatening sky : Janet noticed at once that he was rather pale.

"We will have luncheon as they pull us back," said he, in an absent way, as if he was not quite sure of what was happening around him.

He got her into the boat, and then followed. The men, not sorry to get away from these jagged rocks, took to their oars with a will. And then he sat silent and distraught, as the two women, muffled up in their cloaks, chatted cheerfully, and partook of the sandwiches and claret that Janet had got out of the basket. "*Fhir a bhata*" the men sang to themselves ; and they passed under the great cliffs, all black and thunderous now ; and the white surf was springing over the rocks. Macleod neither ate nor drank ; but sometimes he joined in the conversation in a forced way ; once or twice he laughed more loudly than the occasion seemed to demand.

"Oh yes," he said, "oh yes, you are becoming a good sailor now, Gertrude. You have no longer any fear of the water."

"You will become like little Johnny Wickes, Miss White," the cousin Janet said, "the little boy I showed you the other day. He has got to be like a duck in his love for the water. And indeed I should have thought he would have got a fright when Keith saved him from drowning; but no."

"Did you save him from being drowned?" she said, turning to him. "And you did not tell me the story?"

"It was no story," said he. "He fell into the water; and we picked him up somehow;" and then he turned impatiently to the men, and said some words to them in the Gaelic, and there was no more singing of the Farewell to the Boatman after that.

They got home to Castle Dare before the rain came on—though indeed it was but a passing shower, and it was succeeded by a bright afternoon that deepened into a clear and brilliant sunset; but as they went up through the moist-

smelling larch-wood—and as Janet happened to
fall behind for a moment, to speak to a herd-boy
who was by the way-side—Macleod said to his
companion—

"And have you no other word for me,
Gertrude ? "

Then she said, with a very gracious smile—

" You must be patient, Keith.   Are we not
very well off as we are ?—I know a good many
people who are not quite so well off.   And I
have no doubt we shall have courage to meet
whatever good or bad fortune the days may
bring us; and if it is good, then we shall shake
hands over it, just as the village people do in an
opera."

Fine phrases; though this man, with the dark
and hopeless look in his eyes, did not seem to
gain much gladness from them.   And she forgot
to tell him about that engagement which was to
last till Christmas; perhaps if she had told him
just then he would scarcely have heard her.

CHAPTER V.

THE NEW TRAGEDY.

His generous large nature fought hard to find excuses for her. He strove to convince himself that this strange coldness, this evasion, this half-repellent attitude, was but a form of maiden coyness. It was her natural fear of so great a change. It was the result, perhaps, of some last lingering look back to the scene of her artistic triumphs. It did not even occur to him as a possibility that this woman, with her unstable sympathies and her fatally facile imagination, should have taken up what was now the very end and aim of his life, and have played with the pretty dream, until she grew tired of the toy and was ready to let her wandering fancy turn to something other and new.

He dared not even think of that; but all the same, as he stood at this open window, alone, an unknown fear had come over him. It was a fear altogether vague and undefined; but it seemed to have the power of darkening the daylight around' him. Here was the very picture he had so often desired that she should see—the wind-swept Atlantic; the glad blue skies with their drifting clouds of summer white; the Erisgeir rocks; the green shores of Ulva; and Colonsay, and Gometra, and Staffa all shining in the sunlight; with the sea-birds calling, and the waves breaking, and the soft west wind stirring the fuchsia-bushes below the windows of Castle Dare. And it was all dark now; and the sea was a lonely thing—more lonely than ever it had been even during that long winter that he had said was like a grave.

And she?—at this moment she was down at the small bridge that crossed the burn. She had gone out to seek her father; had found him coming up through the larch-wood; and was now accompanying him back. They had rested here; he sitting on the weather-worn parapet of the bridge; she leaning over it, and idly dropping bits of velvet-green moss into the whirl of clear brown water below.

"I suppose we must be thinking of getting away from Castle Dare, Gerty," said he.

"I shall not be sorry," she answered.

But even Mr. White was somewhat taken aback by the cool promptitude of this reply.

"Well, you know your own business best," he said to her. "It is not for me to interfere. I said from the beginning I would not interfere. But still—I wish you would be a little more explicit, Gerty, and let one understand what you mean—whether, in fact, you do mean, or do not mean, to marry Macleod?"

"And who said that I proposed not to marry him?" said she, but she still leant over the rough stones and looked at the water. "The first thing that would make me decline would be the driving me into a corner—the continual goading, and reminding me of the duty I had to perform. There has been just a little too much of that here"—and at this point she raised herself so that she could regard her father when

she wished—"and I really must say that I do
not like to be taking a holiday with the feeling
hanging over you that certain things are expected
of you every other moment, and that you run
the risk of being considered a very heartless and
ungrateful person unless you do and say certain
things you would perhaps rather not do and say.
I should like to be let alone. I hate being
goaded. And I certainly did not expect that
you too, papa, would try to drive me into a
corner."

She spoke with some little warmth. Mr.
White smiled.

"I was quite unaware, Gerty," said he, "that
you were suffering this fearful persecution."

"You may laugh, but it is true," said she, and
there was a trifle of colour in her cheeks. "The
serious interests I am supposed to be concerned
about! Such profound topics of conversation!
Will the steamer come by the south to-morrow,
or round by the north? The Gometra men have
had a good take of lobsters yesterday. Will the
head-man at the Something lighthouse be trans-
ferred to some other lighthouse; and how will

his wife and family like the change? They are doing very well with the subscription for a bell for the Free Church at Iona. The deer have been down at John Maclean's barley again. Would I like to visit the weaver at Iona who has such a wonderful turn for mathematics; and would I like to know the man at Salen who has the biographies of all the great men of the time in his head?"

Miss White had worked herself up to a pretty pitch of contemptuous indignation; her father was almost beginning to believe that it was real.

"It is all very well for the Macleods to interest themselves with these trumpery little local matters. They play the part of grand patron; the people are proud to honour them; it is a condescension when they remember the name of the crofter's youngest boy. But as for me—when I am taken about—well, I do not like being stared at as if they thought I was wearing too fine clothes. I don't like being continually placed in a position of inferiority through my ignorance—an old fool of a boatman saying 'Bless me!' when I have to admit that

I don't know the difference between luggers
and smacks. I don't want to know. I don't
want to be continually told. I wish these
people would meet me on my own ground. I
wish the Macleods would begin to talk after
dinner about the Lord Chamberlain's interference
with the politics of burlesques; and then perhaps
they would not be so glib. I am tired of
hearing about John Maclean's boat; and Donald
Maclean's horse; and Sandy Maclean's refusal
to pay the road-tax. And as for the drinking
of whisky that these sailors get through—well,
it seems to me that the ordinary condition of
things is reversed here altogether; and if they
ever put up an asylum in Mull, it will be a
lunatic asylum for incurable abstainers."

"Now, now, Gerty," said her father—but
all the same he rather liked to see his daughter
get on her high horse, for she talked with
spirit, and it amused him.—"you must remember that Macleod looks on this as a
holiday-time, and perhaps he may be a little
lax in his regulations. I have no doubt it
is because he is so proud to have you on

board his yacht that he occasionally gives the men an extra glass—and I am sure it does them no harm, for they seem to me to be as much in the water as out of it."

She paid no heed to this protest. She was determined to give free speech to her sense of wrong, and humiliation, and disappointment.

"What has been the great event since ever we came here—the wildest excitement the island can afford?" she said. "The arrival of the pedlar! A snuffy old man comes into the room, with a huge bundle wrapped up in dirty waterproof. Then there is a wild clatter of Gaelic. But suddenly, don't you know, there are one or two glances at me; and the Gaelic stops; and Duncan, or John, or whatever they call him, begins to stammer in English, and I am shown coarse stockings, and bundles of wool, and drugget petticoats, and cotton handkerchiefs. And then Miss Macleod buys a number of things which I know she does not want; and I am looked on as a strange creature because I do not purchase a bundle of wool or a pair of stock-

ings fit for a farmer. The Autolycus of Mull
is not impressive, papa. Oh, but I forgot
the dramatic surprise—that also was to be
an event I have no doubt. I was suddenly
introduced to a child dressed in a kilt; and
I was to speak to him; and I suppose I was
to be profoundly moved when I heard him
speak to me in my own tongue in this out-of-
the-world place. My own tongue! The horrid
little wretch has not an *h*."

"Well, there's no pleasing you, Gerty,"
said he.

"I don't want to be pleased; I want to be
let alone," said she.

But she said this with just a little too
much sharpness; for her father was, after all,
a human being; and it did seem to him to
be too bad that he should be taunted in
this fashion, when he had done his best to
preserve a wholly neutral attitude.

"Let me tell you this, madam," said he,
in a playful manner, but with some decision
in his tone, "that you may live to have the
pride taken out of you. You have had a

good deal of flattery and spoiling; and you
may find out you have been expecting too
much. As for these Macleods here, I will
say this—although I came here very much
against my own inclination—that I defy any
one to have been more kind, and courteous,
and attentive than they have been to you. I
don't care. It is not my business, as I tell
you. But I must say, Gerty, that when you
make a string of complaints as the only
return for all their hospitality—their exces-
sive and almost burdensome hospitality—I
think that even I am bound to say a word.
You forget how you come here. You, a
perfect stranger, come here as engaged to
marry the old lady's only son—to dispossess
her—very probably to make impossible a
match that she had set her heart on. And
both she and her niece—you understand what
I mean—instead of being cold, or at least
formal, to you, seem to me to think of
nothing from morning till night but how to
surround you with kindness, in a way that
Englishwomen would never think of. And

this you call persecution; and you are vexed with them because they won't talk to you about theatres—why, bless my soul, how long is it since you were yourself talking about theatres as if the very word choked you!——"

"Well, at least, papa, I never thought you would turn against me," said she, as she put her head partly aside, and made a mouth as if she were about to cry; "and when mamma made you promise to look after Carry and me, I am sure she never thought——"

Now this was too much for Mr. White. In the small eyes behind those big gold spectacles there was a quick flash of fire.

"Don't be a fool, Gerty," said he, in downright anger. "You know it is no use your trying to humbug me. If you think the ways of this house are too poor and mean for your grand notions of state; if you think he has not enough money, and you are not likely to have fine dinners and entertainments for your friends; if you are determined to break off the match—why, then do it!—but, I tell you, don't try to humbug me!"

Miss White's pathetic attitude suddenly vanished. She drew herself up with much dignity and composure, and said—

"At all events, sir, I have been taught my duty to you; and I think it better not to answer you."

With that she moved off towards the house; and Mr. White, taking to whistling, began to do as she had been doing—idly throwing bits of moss into the rushing burn. After all, it was none of his business.

But that evening, some little time before dinner, it was proposed they should go for a stroll down to the shore; and then it was that Miss White thought she would seize the occasion to let Macleod know of her arrangements for the coming autumn and winter. Ordinarily, on such excursions, she managed to walk with Janet Macleod—the old lady of Castle Dare seldom joined them—leaving Macleod to follow with her father; but this time she so managed it that Macleod and she left the house together. Was he greatly over-joyed? There was a constrained and anxious

look on his face that had been there too much
of late.

"I suppose Oscar is more at home here than
in Bury Street, St. James's?" said she, as the
handsome collie went down the path before
them.

"No doubt," said he, absently: he was not
thinking of any collie.

"What beautiful weather we are having," said
she, to this silent companion. "It is always
changing, but always beautiful. There is only
one other aspect I should like to see—the snow-
time."

"We have not much snow here," said he. "It
seldom lies in the winter."

This was a strange conversation for two
engaged lovers: it was not much more in-
teresting than their talk—how many ages ago?
—at Charing Cross station. But then, when
she had said to him, "*Ought we to take
tickets?*" she had looked into his face with
those appealing, innocent, beautiful eyes. Now
her eyes never met his. She was afraid.

She managed to lead up to her announcement

AN EVENING WALK.

To face p. 96, vol. iii.

skilfully enough. By the time they reached the shore an extraordinarily beautiful sunset was shining over the sea and the land—something so bewildering and wonderful that they all four stopped to look at it. The Atlantic was a broad expanse of the palest and most brilliant green, with the pathway of the sun a flashing line of gold coming right across until it met the rocks, and these were a jet black against the glow. Then the distant islands of Colonsay, and Staffa, and Lunga, and Fladda, lying on this shining green sea, appeared to be of a perfectly trans- parent bronze; while nearer at hand the long ranges of cliffs were becoming a pale rose-red under the darkening blue-grey sky. It was a blaze of colour such as she had never even dreamed of as being possible in nature; nothing she had as yet seen in these northern latitudes had at all approached it. And as she stood there, and looked at those transparent islands of bronze on the green sea, she said to him—

"Do you know, Keith, this is not at all like the place I had imagined as the scene of the gloomy stories you used to tell me about the

revenges of the clans. I have been frightened
once or twice since I came here, no doubt—by
the wild sea and the darkness of the cathedral,
and so forth; but the longer I stay the less I see
to suggest those awful stories. How could you
associate such an evening as this with a frightful
tragedy? Do you think those people ever
existed who were supposed to have suffocated,
or slaughtered, or starved to death any one who
opposed their wishes?"

"And I do not suppose they troubled themselves much about fine sunsets," said he. "That
was not what they had to think about in those
days."

"Perhaps not," said she, lightly; "but, you
know, I had expected to find a place from which
I could gain some inspiration for tragedy—for I
should like to try, once for all—if I *should* have
to give up the stage—whether I had the stuff of
a tragic actress in me. And, you know, in that
case, I ought to dress in black velvet; and carry
a taper through dungeons; and get accustomed
to storms, and gloom, and thunder and lightning."

"We have no appliances here for the education of an actress—I am very sorry," said he.

"Now, Keith, that is hardly fair," said she, with a smile. "You know it is only a trial. And you saw what they said of my *Juliet*. Oh, did I tell you about the new tragedy that is coming out?"

"No, I do not think you did," said he.

"Ah, well, it is a great secret as yet; but there is no reason why you should not hear of it."

"I am not anxious to hear of it," said he, without any rudeness.

"But it concerns me," she said, "and so I must tell you. It is written by a brother of Mr. Lemuel, the artist I have often spoken to you about. He is by profession an architect; but if this play should turn out to be as fine as some people say it is, he ought to take to dramatic writing. In fact all the Lemuels—there are three brothers of them, you know—are like Michael Angelo and Leonardo—artists to the finger-tips, in every direction—poets, painters, sculptors and all the rest of it. And I do think

H 2

I ought to feel flattered by their choice in asking me to play the heroine ; for so much depends on the choice of the actress——"

"And you are still to act ?" said he, quickly, though he spoke in a low voice, so that those behind should not hear.

"Surely I explained to you ?" said she, in a pleasant manner. "After all, life-long habits are not so easily cast aside ; and I knew you would be generous, and bear with me a little bit, Keith."

He turned to her. The glow of the sunset caught his face. There was a strange, hopeless sadness in his eyes.

"Generous to you ?" said he. "You know I would give you my life if that would serve you. But this is worse than taking my life from me."

"Keith, Keith !" said she, in gentle protest, "I don't know what you mean. You should not take things so seriously. What is it after all ? It was as an actress that you knew me first. What is the difference of a few months more or less ? If I had not been an actress, you would never have known me—do you recollect that? By the way, has Major Stewart's wife got a piano ?"

He turned and stared at her for a second, in a bewildered way.

"Oh yes," said he, with a laugh, "Mrs. Stewart has got a piano. She has got a very good piano. And what is the song you would sing now, sweetheart? Shall we finish up and have done with it, with a song at the end? That is the way in the theatre, you know—a dance and a song as the people go. And what shall our song be now? There was one that Norman Ogilvie used to sing."

"I don't know why you should talk to me like that, Keith," said she, though she seemed somewhat frightened by this fierce gaiety. "I was going to tell you that, if Mrs. Stewart had a piano, I would very gladly sing one or two songs for your mother and Miss Macleod when we went over there to-morrow. You have frequently asked me. Indeed I have brought with me the very songs I sang to you the first time I saw you—at Mrs. Ross's."

Instantly his memory flew back to that day— to the hushed little room over the sunlit gardens —to the beautiful, gentle, sensitive girl who

seemed to have so strange an interest in the
Highlands—to the wonderful thrill that went
through him when she began to sing with an
exquisite pathos "A wee bird cam' to our ha'
door"—and to the prouder enthusiasm that
stirred him when she sang "I'll to Lochiel, and
Appin, and kneel to them!" These were fine,
and tender, and proud songs. There was no
gloom about them—nothing about a grave and
the dark winter-time, and a faithless lost love.
This song of Norman Ogilvie's that he had gaily
proposed they should sing now? What had
Major Stewart, or his wife, or any one in Mull
to do with "Death's black wine"?

"I meant to tell you, Keith," said she, somewhat nervously, "that I had signed an engagement
to remain at the Piccadilly Theatre till Christmas
next. I knew you wouldn't mind—I mean, you
would be considerate, and you would understand
how difficult it is for one to break away all at
once from one's old associations. And then, you
know, Keith," said she, shyly, "though you may
not like the theatre, you ought to be proud of my
success, as even my friends and acquaintances

are. And as they are all anxious to see me make another appearance in tragedy, I really should like to try it; so that when my portrait appears in the Academy next year, people may not be saying, 'Look at the impertinence of that girl appearing as a tragic actress when she can do nothing beyond the familiar modern comedy!' I should have told you all about it before, Keith, but I know you hate to hear any talk about the theatre; and I sha'n't bore you again, you may depend on that. Isn't it time to go back now? See! the rose-colour is away from Ulva now; it is quite a dark purple."

He turned in silence and led the way back. Behind them he could faintly hear Mr. White discoursing to Janet Macleod about the manner in which the old artists mixed their own pigments.

Then Macleod said with a great gentleness and restraint,—

"And when you go away from here, Gertrude, I suppose I must say good-bye to you; and no one knows when we shall see each other again. You are returning to the theatre. If that is

your wish, I would not try to thwart it. You
know best what is the highest prize the world can
give you. And how can I warn you against
failure and disappointment? I know you will be
successful. I know the people will applaud you,
and your head will be filled with their praises.
You are going forward to a new triumph, Gerty;
and the first step you will take—will be on my
heart."

CHAPTER VI.

AN UNDERSTANDING.

"Papa dear," said Miss White to her father, in a playful way, although it was a serious sort of playfulness, "I have a vague feeling that there is a little too much electricity in the atmosphere of this place just at present. I am afraid there may be an explosion; and you know my nerves can't stand much of a shock. I should be glad to get away."

By this time she had quite made up that little difference with her father—she did not choose to be left alone at a somewhat awkward crisis. She had told him she was sure he had not meant what he said about her; and she had expressed her sorrow for having provoked him; and there an end. And if Mr. White had been driven by his anger to be for the moment the ally of

Macleod, he was not disinclined to take the other side now and let Miss White have her own will. The vast amount of training he had bestowed on her through many long years was not to be thrown away after all.

"I told him last night," said she, "of my having signed an engagement till Christmas next."

"Oh, indeed," said her father, quickly looking at her over his spectacles.

"Yes," said she, thoughtfully, "and he was not so disturbed or angry as I had expected. Not at all. He was very kind about it. But I don't understand him."

"What do you not understand?"

"He has grown so strange of late—so sombre. Once, you know, he was the lightest-hearted young man—enjoying every minute of his life, you know—and really, papa, I think——"

And here Miss White stopped.

"At all events," said she, quickly, "I want to be in a less dangerously excited atmosphere, where I can sit down and consider matters calmly. It was much better when he and I corresponded; then we could fairly learn what each other thought. Now I am almost afraid of him—I mean I am afraid to ask him a question. I have to keep out of his way. And if it comes to that, papa, you know, I feel now as if I was called on to act a part from morning till night, whereas I was always assured that if I left the stage and married him it was to be my natural self and I should have no more need to pose and sham. However, that is an old quarrel between you and me, and we will put it aside. What's more to the purpose is this— it was half understood that when we left Castle Dare he was to come with us through at least a part of the Highlands."

"There was a talk of it."

"Don't you think," said Miss White, with some little hesitation, and with her eyes cast down, "don't you think that would be—a little inconvenient— ? "

"I should say that was for you to decide," he answered, somewhat coldly; for it was too bad that she should be continually asking his advice and then openly disregarding it.

"I should think it would be a little un-
comfortable," she said, demurely. "I fancy
he has taken that engagement till Christmas a
little more to heart than he chooses to reveal—
that is natural—I knew it would be a disappointment—but then, you know, papa, the temptation was very great, and I had almost promised
the Lemuels to do what I could for the piece.
And if I am to give up the stage, wouldn't it be
fine to wind up with a blaze of fireworks to
astonish the public ? "

"Are you so certain you will astonish the
public ?" her father said.

"I have the courage to try," she answered,
readily. "And you are not going to throw cold
water on my endeavours, are you, papa ? Well,
as I was saying, it is perhaps natural for
Sir Keith to feel a bit annoyed; and I am
afraid if he went travelling with us, we should
be continually skating on the edge of a quarrel.
Besides, to tell you the truth, papa—with all
his kindness and gentleness, there is sometimes
about him a sort of intensity that I scarcely like
—it makes me afraid of him. If it were on the

stage, I should say it was a splendid piece of acting—of the suppressed vehement kind, you know; but really—during a holiday-time, when one naturally wishes to enjoy the fine weather and gather strength for one's work — well, I do think he ought not to come with us, papa."

"Very well, you can hint as much without being rude."

"I was thinking," said she, "of the Mr. and Mrs. Bald who were in that Newcastle company, and who went to Aberdeen. Do you remember them, papa?"

"The low comedian, you mean?"

"Yes. Well, at all events they would be glad to see us. And so—don't you think— we could let Macleod understand that we were going to see some friends in the north? Then he would not think of coming with us."

"The representation would scarcely be justifiable," observed Mr. White, with a profound air, "in ordinary circumstances. But, as you say, it would be neither for his comfort nor for yours that he should go with us."

"Comfort!" she exclaimed. "Much comfort I have had since I came here! Comfort I call quiet, and being let alone. Another fortnight at this place would give me brain-fever—your life continually in danger either on the sea or by the cliffs—your feelings supposed to be always up at passion pitch—it is all a whirl of secret or declared emotions that don't give you a moment's rest. Oh, papa, won't it be nice to have a day or two's quiet in our own home, with Carry and Marie! And you know Mr. Lemuel will be in town all the summer and winter. The material for *his* work he finds within himself. He doesn't need to scamper off like the rest of them to hunt out picturesque peasants and studies of waterfalls—trotting about the country with a note-book in hand——"

"Gerty, Gerty," said her father with a smile, "your notions are unformed on that subject. What have I told you often—that the artist is only a reporter. Whether he uses the pencil, or the pen, or his own face and voice to express the highest thoughts and emotions of which he is conscious, he is only a reporter—a penny-a-

liner whose words are written in fire. And you
—don't you carry your note-book too?"

"I was not comparing myself with an artist
like Mr. Lemuel, papa. No, no. Of course
I have to keep my eyes open, and pick up
things that may be useful. His work is the
work of intense spiritual contemplation—it is
inspiration——"

"No doubt," the father said, "the inspiration
of Botticelli."

"Papa!"

Mr. White chuckled to himself. He was not
given to joking: an epigram was not in conso-
nance with his high sententiousness. But instantly he resumed his solemn deportment.

"A picture is as much a part of the world
as a human face: why should I not take my
inspiration from a picture as well as from a
human face?"

"You mean to say he is only a copyist—a
plagiarist!" she said, with some indignation.

"Not at all," said he. "All artists have their
methods founded more or less on the methods
of those who have gone before them. You don't

expect an artist to discover for himself an
entirely new principle of art, any more than
you expect him to paint in pigments of his
own invention. Mr. Lemuel has been a diligent
student of Botticelli—that is all."

This strange talk amid the awful loneliness
and grandeur of Glen Sloich! They were idly
walking along the rough road : far above them
rose the giant slopes of the mountains retreating
into heavy masses of cloud that were moved by
the currents of the morning wind. It was a
grey day; and the fresh-water lake here was of
a leaden hue ; and the browns and greens of the
mountain-side were dark and intense. There
was no sign of human life or habitation ; there
was no bird singing; the deer were far away in
the unknown valleys above them, hidden by the
mystic cloud-phantoms. There was an odour of
sweet-gale in the air. The only sound was the
murmuring of the streams that were pouring
down through these vast solitudes to the sea.

And now they reached a spot from whence, on
turning, they caught sight of the broad plain of
the Atlantic—all wind-swept and white. And

the sky was dark and low down; though at one
place the clouds had parted, and there was a
glimmer of blue as narrow and keen as the edge
of a knife. But there were showers about; for
Iona was invisible, and Staffa was faintly grey
through the passing rain; and Ulva was almost
black as the storm approached in its gloom.
Botticelli! Those men now in that small lug-
sailed boat—far away off the point of Gometra—
a tiny dark thing apparently lost every second or
so amid the white Atlantic surge—and wrestling
hard with the driving wind and sea to reach the
thundering and foam-filled caverns of Staffa—
they were not thinking much of Botticelli.
Keith Macleod was in that boat. The evening
before Miss White had expressed some light wish
about some trifle or other; but had laughingly
said that she must wait till she got back to the
region of shops. Unknown to her, Macleod had
set off to intercept the steamer : and he would
go on board and get hold of the steward ; and
would the steward be so kind as to hunt about
in Oban to see if that trifle could not be found ?
Macleod would not intrust so important a

message to any one else : he would himself go
out to meet the *Pioneer*.

"The sky is becoming very dark," Mr.
White said ; "we had better go back, Gerty."

But before they had gone far, the first
heavy drops were beginning to fall, and they
were glad to run for refuge to some great
grey boulders which lay in the moist moorland
at the foot of the mountain-slopes.　In the
lee of these rocks they were in comparative
safety ; and they waited patiently until the
gale of wind and rain should pass over.　And
what were these strange objects that appeared
in the grey mists far along the valley ?　She
touched her father's arm—she did not speak ;
it was her first sight of a herd of red-deer,
and as the deer had doubtless been startled
by a shepherd or his dog, they were making
across the glen at a good speed.　First came
the hinds, running almost in Indian file, and
then with a longer stride came one or two
stags, their antlered heads high in the air, as
though they were listening for sounds behind
them and sniffing the wind in front of them

at the same time. But so far away were they
that they were only blurred objects passing
through the rain-mists; they passed across
like swift ghosts; there was no sound heard
at all. And then the rain ceased, and the
air grew warm around them. They came
out from the shadow of the rock—behold! a
blaze of hot sun on the moist moors, with a
sudden odour of bracken, and young heather,
and sweet-gale all about them. And the sandy
road quickly grew dry again; and the heavens
opened; and there was a flood of sunlight
falling on that rushing and breezy Atlantic.
They walked back to Dare.

"Tuesday, then, shall we say, papa?" she
remarked, just before entering.

"Very well."

"And we are going to see some friends in
Aberdeen."

"Very well."

After this Miss White became a great deal
more cheerful; and she was very complaisant
to them all at luncheon. And quite by accident she asked Macleod, who had returned

by this time, whether they talked Scotch in
Aberdeen.

"Because, you know," said she, "one should
always be learning on one's travels; and many
a time I have heard people disputing about
the pronunciation of the Scotch; and one
ought to be able to read Burns with a proper
accent. Now you have no Scotch at all here;
you don't say 'my dawtie,' and 'ben the
hoose,' and 'twixt the gloaming and the mirk.'

"Oh no," said he, "we have none of the
Scotch at all, except among those who have
been for a time to Glasgow or Greenock; and
our own language, the Gaelic, is unknown to
strangers; and our way of speaking English
—that is only made a thing to laugh at.
And yet I do not laugh at all at the blunders
of our poor people in a strange tongue. You
may laugh at our poor people for their way of
speaking English—the accent of it and their
mistakes; but then other people sometimes
make mistakes too in a strange tongue. Did
you ever hear of the poor Highlander who
was asked how he had been employing him-

self, and, after a long time, he said, 'I wass for tree years a herring-fish, and I wass for four months or tree months a broke stone on the road?' Perhaps the Highlanders are not very clever at picking up another language; but all the same that did not prevent their going to all parts of the world and fighting the battles of other people. And do you know that in Canada there are descendants of the Highlanders who went there in the last century—and they are proud of their name and their history—and they have swords that were used at Prestonpans and Culloden— but these Macnabs, and Mackays, and MacNeils they speak only French! But I think, if they have Highland blood in them, and if they were to hear the '*Fàilte Phrionnsa*' played on the pipes, they would recognise that language. And why were you asking about Aberdeen?"

"That is not a Highland, but a Scotch way of answering my question," said she, smiling.

"Oh, I beg your pardon," said he, hastily,

"but indeed I have never been to Aberdeen,
and I do not know what it is they speak
there, but I should say it was likely to be a
mixture of Scotch and English such as all
the big towns have. I do not think it is a
Highland place, like Inverness."

"Now I will answer your question," said
she. "I asked you because papa and I
propose to go there before returning to England——."

How quickly the light fell from his face!

"——the fact is, we have some friends
there."

There was silence. They all felt that it
was for Macleod to speak; and they may
have been guessing as to what was passing
in his mind. But to their surprise he said,
in almost a gay fashion—

"Ah, well, you know they accuse us Highland
folk of being rather too importunate as hosts;
but we will try not to harass you; and if you
have friends in Aberdeen, it would not be fair to
beg of you to leave them aside this time. But
surely you are not thinking of going to Aberdeen

yet, when there is many a place you have yet to
see about here. I was to take you in the *Umpire*
to Skye; and we had many a talk about the
Lewis too."

"Thank you very much," said she demurely.
"I am sure you have been most kind to us;
but—the fact is—I think we must leave on
Tuesday."

"On Tuesday!" said he; but it was only for
an instant that he winced. Again he roused
himself—for he was talking in the presence of
his mother and the cousin Janet—"You have
not been quite fair to us," said he, cheerfully;
"you have not given yourself time to make our
acquaintance. Are you determined to go away
as you came, the Fionaghal? But then, you
know, Fionaghal came and stayed among us,
before she began to write her songs about the
western isles; and the next time you come, that
must be for a longer time, and you will get to
know us all better, and we will not frighten you
any more by taking you on the sea at night or
into the cathedral ruins. Ah!" said he, with
a smile lighting up his face—but it was a

constrained gaiety altogether. "Do I know now
why you are hurrying away so soon? You want
to avoid that trip in the *Umpire* to the island
where I used to think I would like my grave to
be——"

"Keith!" said Lady Macleod with a frown.
"How can you repeat that nonsense! Miss
White will think you are mad!"

"It was only an old fancy, mother," said he,
gently. "And we were thinking of going out to
one of the Treshnish islands, anyway. Surely it
is a harmless thing that a man should choose out
the place of his own grave, so long as he does
not want to be put into it too soon."

"It will be time for you to speak of such
things thirty years hence," said Lady Macleod.

"Thirty years is a long time," said he; and
then he added, lightly, "but if we do not go
out to the Treshnish islands we must go somewhere else before the Tuesday; and would you
go round to Loch Sunart now; or shall we drive
you to-morrow to see Glen More and Carsaig?
Then you must not leave Mull without visiting our
beautiful town—and capital—that is Tobermory."

Every one was quite surprised and pleased to find Macleod taking the sudden departure of his sweetheart in this fashion; it showed that he had abundant confidence in the future. And if Miss White had her own thoughts about the matter, it was at all events satisfactory to her that outwardly Macleod and she were parting on good terms.

But that evening he happened to find her alone for a few moments; and all the constrained cheerfulness had left his eyes, and there was a dark look there—of hopeless anxiety and pain.

"I do not wish to force you, Gerty—to persecute you," said he." You are our guest. But before you go away, cannot you give me one definite word of promise and hope—only one word?"

"I am quite sure you don't want to persecute me, Keith," said she, "but you should remember there is a long time of waiting before us, and there will be plenty of opportunity for explaining and arranging everything when we have leisure to write——"

"To write!" he exclaimed. "But I am

coming to see you, Gerty! Do you think I
could go through another series of long months,
with only those letters, and letters, and letters,
to break one's heart over? I could not do it
again, Gerty. And when you have visited your
friends in Aberdeen, I am coming to London."

"Why, Keith, there is the shooting!"

"I do not think I shall try the shooting this
year—it is an anxiety—I cannot have patience
with it. I am coming to London, Gerty."

"Oh, very well, Keith," said she, with an
affectation of cheerful content; "then there is no
use in our taking a solemn good-bye just now—is
there? You know how I hate scenes. And we
shall part very good friends, shall we not? And
when you come to London, we shall make up all
our little differences, and have everything on a
clear understanding. Is it a bargain? Here
comes your cousin Janet—now show her that we
are good friends, Keith! And for goodness'
sake don't say that you mean to give up your
shooting this year, or she will wonder what I
have made of you. Give up your shooting!
Why, a woman would as soon give up her right

of being incomprehensible and whimsical and capricious—her right of teasing people, as I very much fear I have been teasing you, Keith. But it will be all set right when you come to London."

And from that moment to the moment of her departure, Miss White seemed to breathe more freely, and she took less care to avoid Keith Macleod in her daily walks and ways. There was at last quite a good understanding between them, as the people around imagined.

CHAPTER VII.

AFRAID.

But the very first thing she did on reaching home again was to write to Macleod begging him to postpone his visit to London. What was the use? The company of which she formed a part was most probably going on an autumn tour; she was personally very busy. Surely it would not much interest him to be present at the production of a new piece in Liverpool?

And then she pointed out to him that, as she had her duties and occupations, so ought he to have. It was monstrous his thought of foregoing the shooting that year. Why, if he wanted some additional motive, what did he say to preserving as much grouse-plumage as would trim a cloak for her? It was a great pity that the skins of so beautiful a bird should be thrown

away. And she desired him to present her kind
regards to Lady Macleod and to Miss Macleod;
and to thank them both for their great kindness.

Immediately after writing that letter, Miss
White seemed to grow very light-hearted indeed,
and she laughed and chatted with Carry, and
was exceedingly affectionate towards her sister.

"And what do you think of your own home
now, Gerty?" said Miss Carry, who had been
making some small experiments in arrangement.

"You mean, after my being among the
savages?" said she. "Ah, it is too true,
Carry. I have seen them in their war-paint;
and I have shuddered at their spears; and I have
made voyages in their canoes. But it is worth
while going anywhere and doing anything in
order to come back and experience such a sense
of relief and quiet. Oh, what a delicious cushion!
—where did you get it, Carry?"

She sank back in the rocking-chair out on this
shaded verandah. It was the slumbering noon-
tide of a July day; the foliage above and about
the Regent's Canal hung motionless in the still
sunlight; and there was a perfume of roses in

the air.   Here, at last, was repose.   She had
said that her notion of happiness was to be let
alone ; and—now that she had despatched that
forbidding letter—she would be able to enjoy a
quiet and languor free from care.

"Aha, Gerty, don't you know ? " said the
younger sister.   "Well, I suppose, you poor
creature, you don't know—you have been among
the tigers and crocodiles so long.   That cushion
is a present from Mr. Lemuel to me—to me,
mind, not to you—and he brought it all the way
from Damascus some years ago.   Oh, Gerty, if
I was only three years older, shouldn't I like
to be your rival, and have a fight with you
for him !"

"I don't know what you mean !" said the
elder sister, sharply.

"Oh, don't you !   Poor, innocent thing !
Well, I am not going to quarrel with you this
time—for at last you are showing some sense.
How you ever could have thought of Mr. Howson,
or Mr. Brook, or—you know whom—I never
could imagine ; but here is some one now whom
people have heard of—some one with fame like

yourself—who will understand you. Oh, Gerty, hasn't he lovely eyes?"

"Like a gazelle," said the other. "You know what Mr. —— said—that he never met the appealing look of Mr. Lemuel's eyes without feeling in his pockets for a biscuit."

"He wouldn't say anything like that about you, Gerty," Carry said, reproachfully.

"Who wouldn't?"

"Mr. Lemuel."

"Oh, Carry, don't you understand that I am so glad to be allowed to talk nonsense? I have been all strung up, lately, like the string of a violin. Everything *au grand sérieux.* I want to be idle, and to chat, and to talk nonsense. Where did you get that bunch of stephanotis?"

"Mr. Lemuel brought it last evening. He knew you were coming home to-day. Oh, Gerty, do you know I have seen your portrait, though it isn't finished yet; and you look—you look like an inspired prophetess. I never saw anything so lovely!"

"Indeed," said Miss White, with a smile; but she was pleased.

"When the public see that, they will know what you are really like, Gerty—instead of buying your photograph in a shop from a collection of ballet-dancers and circus-women. That is where you ought to be—in the Royal Academy : not in a shop window with any mountebank. Oh, Gerty, do you know who is your latest rival in the stationer's windows? The woman who dresses herself as a mermaid and swims in a transparent tank, below water. Fin-fin they call her. I suppose you have not been reading the newspapers!"

"Not much."

"There is a fine collection for you up stairs. And there is an article about you, in the *Islington Young Men's Improvement Association Journal.* It is signed *Trismegistus.* Oh, it is beautiful, Gerty—quite full of poetry! It says you are an enchantress striking the rockiest heart, and a well of pure emotion springs up. It says you have the beauty of Mrs. Siddons and the genius of Rachel."

"Dear me!"

"Ah, you don't half believe in yourself,

Gerty," said the younger sister, with a critical air. "It is the weak point about you. You depreciate yourself, and you make light of other people's belief in you. However, you can't go against your own genius. That is too strong for you. As soon as you get on the stage, then you forget to laugh at yourself."

"Really, Carry, has papa been giving you a lecture about me?"

"Oh, laugh away; but you know it is true. And a woman like you—you were going to throw yourself away on a ——"

"Carry! There are some things that are better not talked about," said Gertrude White, curtly, as she rose and went in-doors.

Miss White betook herself to her professional and domestic duties with much alacrity and content, for she believed that by her skill as a letter-writer she could easily ward off the importunities of her too passionate lover. It is true that at times, and in despite of her playful evasion, she was visited by a strange dread. However far away, the cry of a strong man in

his agony has something terrible in it. And
what was this he wrote to her in simple and
calm words ?—

"Are our paths diverging, Gerty? and, if
that is so, what will be the end of it for me
and for you? Are you going away from me?
After all that has passed, are we to be separated
in the future, and you will go one way, and I
must go the other way, with all the world between us, so that I shall never see you again?
Why will you not speak? You hint of lingering
doubts and hesitations. Why have you not the
courage to be true to yourself—to be true to
your woman's heart—to take your life in your
own hands and shape it so that it shall be
worthy of you?"

Well, she did speak, in answer to this
piteous prayer. She was a skilful letter-
writer.

"It may seem very ungrateful in an actress,
you know, .dear Keith, to contest the truth of
anything said by Shakespere; but I don't think,
with all humility, there ever was so much nonsense put into so small a space as there is in

these lines that everybody quotes at your head—

> 'To thine own self be true;
> And it must follow, as the night the day,
> Thou canst not then be false to any man.'

'Be true to yourself,' people say to you. But surely every one who is conscious of failings, and deceitfulness, and unworthy instincts, would rather try to be a little better than himself? Where else would there be any improvement, in an individual, or in society? You have to fight against yourself, instead of blindly yielding to your wish of the moment. I know I, for one, should not like to trust myself. I wish to be better than I am—to be other than I am—and I naturally look around for help and guidance. Then you find people recommending you absolutely diverse ways of life, and with all show of authority and reason, too; and in such an important matter ought not one to consider carefully before making a final choice?"

Miss White's studies in mental and moral science, as will readily be perceived, had not been of a profound character. But he did not stay to detect the obvious fallacy of her argument. It was all a maze of words to him. The drowning man does not hear questions addressed to him. He only knows that the waters are closing over him—and that there is no arm stretched out to save.

"I do not know myself for two minutes together," she wrote. "What is my present mood, for example? Why, one of absolute and ungovernable hatred—hatred of the woman who would take my place if I were to retire from the stage. I have been thinking of it all the morning—picturing myself as an unknown nonentity, vanished from the eyes of the public, in a social grave. And I have to listen to people praising the new actress; and I have to read columns about her in the papers; and I am unable to say, 'Why all that and more was written and said about me!' What has an actress to show for herself if once she leaves the stage? People forget her the next day; no record is kept of her triumphs. A painter now, who spends years of his life in earnest study—it does not matter to him whether the public applaud or not, whether they forget or not. He has always before him these evidences of his genius; and among his friends he can choose his fit audience. Even when he is an old man, and listening to the praises of all the young fellows who have caught the taste of the public, he can at all events show something of his work as testimony of what he was. But an actress, the moment she leaves the stage, is a snuffed-out candle. She has her stage-dresses to prove that she acted certain parts; and she may have a scrap-book with cuttings of criticisms from the provincial papers! You know, dear Keith, all this is very heart-sickening; and I am quite aware that it will trouble you—as it troubles me, and sometimes makes me ashamed of myself—but then it is true, and it is better for both of us that it should be known. I could not undertake to be a hypocrite all my life. I must confess to you, whatever be the consequences, that I distinctly made a mistake when I thought it was such an easy thing to adopt a whole new set of opinions and tastes and habits. The old Adam, as your Scotch ministers would say, keeps coming back to jog my elbow as an old familiar

friend. And you would not have me conceal
the fact from you? I know how difficult it will
be for you to understand or sympathise with me.
You have never been brought up to a profession,
every inch of your progress in which you have
to contest against rivals; and you don't know
how jealous one is of one's position when it is
gained. I think I would rather be made an old
woman of sixty to-morrow morning than et gup
and go out and find my name printed in small
letters in the theatre-bills. And if I try to
imagine what my feelings would be if I were
to retire from the stage, surely that is in your
interest as well as mine. How would you like
to be tied for life to a person who was continually looking back to her past career with
regret, and who was continually looking around
her for objects of jealous and envious anger?
Really, I try to do my duty by everybody. All
the time I was at Castle Dare I tried to picture
myself living there, and taking an interest in
the fishing, and the farms and so on; and if
I was haunted by the dread that, instead of
thinking about the fishing and the farms, I

should be thinking of the triumphs of the actress who had taken my place in the attention of the public, I had to recognise the fact. It is wretched and pitiable, no doubt; but look at my training. If you tell me to be true to myself—that· is myself. At all events I feel more contented that I have made a frank confession."

Surely it was a fair and reasonable letter? But the answer that came to it had none of its pleasant common sense. It was all a wild appeal —a calling on her not to fall away from the resolves she had made—not to yield to those despondent moods. There was but the one way to get rid of her doubts and hesitations; let her at once cast aside the theatre and all its associations and malign influences, and become his wife, and he would take her by the hand, and lead her away from that besetting temptation. Could she forget the day on which she gave him the red rose? She was a woman; she could not forget.

She .folded up the letter; and held. it in her hand; and went into her father's room. There

was a certain petulant and irritated look on her
face.

"He says he is coming up to London, papa,"
said she, abruptly.

"I suppose you mean Sir Keith Macleod,"
said he.

"Well, of course. And can you imagine anything more provoking—just at present, when we
are rehearsing this new play, and when all the
time I can afford Mr. Lemuel wants for the
portrait? I declare the only time I feel quiet,
secure, safe from the interference of anybody
—and more especially the worry of the post-
man—is when I am having that portrait painted;
the intense stillness of the studio is delightful,
and you have beautiful things all around you.
As soon as I open the door, I come out into the
world again, with constant vexations and appre-
hensions all around. Why, I don't know but
that at any minute Sir Keith Macleod may
come walking up to the gate!"

"And why should that possibility keep you
in terror?" said her father, calmly.

"Well, not in terror," said she, looking down,

"but—but anxiety, at least; and a very great deal of anxiety. Because I know he will want explanations and promises, and I don't know what—just at the time I am most worried and unsettled about everything I mean to do."

Her father regarded her for a second or two.

"Well?" said he.

"Isn't that enough?" she said, with some indignation.

"Oh," said he, coldly, "you have merely come to me to pour out your tale of wrongs. You don't want me to interfere, I suppose. Am I to condole with you?"

"I don't know why you should speak to me like that, at all events," said she.

"Well, I will tell you," he responded, in the same cool, matter-of-fact way. "When you told me you meant to give up the theatre and marry Sir Keith Macleod, my answer was that you were likely to make a mistake. I thought you were a fool to throw away your position as an actress; but I did not urge the point. I merely left the matter in your own hands. Well, you went your own way. For a time your head was

filled with romance—Highland chiefs, and gillies,
and red-deer, and baronial halls, and all that
stuff; and no doubt you persuaded that young
man that you believed in the whole thing fer-
vently, and there was no end to the names you
called theatres and everybody connected with
them.   Not only that, but you must needs drag
me up to the Highlands to pay a visit to a
number of strangers with whom both you and
I lived on terms of apparent hospitality and
goodwill, but in reality on terms of very great
restraint.   Very well.   You begin to discover
that your romance was a little bit removed from
the actual state of affairs—at least, you say
so"——

"I say so!" she exclaimed.

"Hear me out," the father said, patiently.
"I don't want to offend you, Gerty, but I wish
to speak plainly.   You have an amazing faculty
for making yourself believe anything that suits
you.   I have not the least doubt but that you
have persuaded yourself that the change in
your manner towards Keith Macleod was owing
to your discovering that their way of life was

different from what you expected; or perhaps that you still had a lingering fancy for the stage—anything you like. I say you could make yourself believe anything. But I must point out to you that any acquaintance of yours —an outsider—would probably look on the marked attentions Mr. Lemuel has been paying you; and on your sudden conversion to the art-theories of himself and his friends; and on the revival of your ambitious notions about tragedy——"

"You need say no more," said she, with her face grown quickly red, and with a certain proud impatience in her look.

"Oh, yes, but I mean to say more," her father said, quietly, "unless you wish to leave the room. I mean to say this—that when you have persuaded yourself somehow that you would rather reconsider your promise to Sir Keith Macleod — am I right? — it does seem rather hard that you should grow ill-tempered, with him, and accuse him of being the author of your troubles and vexations. I am no great friend of his—I disliked his coming

here at the outset; but I must say that he is a
manly young fellow, and I know he would not
try to throw the blame of any change in his
own sentiments on to some one else. And
another thing I mean to say is—that your
playing the part of the injured Griselda is not
quite becoming, Gerty: at all events, I have
no sympathy with it. If you come and tell
me frankly that you have grown tired of
Macleod, and wish somehow to break your
promise to him, then I can advise you."

"And what would you advise, then," said
she, with equal calmness, "supposing that you
choose to throw all the blame on me?"

"I would say that it is a woman's privilege
to be allowed to change her mind; and that the
sooner you told him so the better."

"Very simple!" she said, with a flavour of
sarcasm in her tone. "Perhaps you don't know
that man as I know him."

"Then you *are* afraid of him?"

She was silent.

"These are certainly strange relations between
two people who talk of getting married. But,

in any case, he cannot suffocate you in a cave,
for you live in London; and in London it is
only an occasional young man about Shoreditch
who smashes his sweetheart with a poker when
she proposes to marry somebody else. He
might, it is true, summon you for breach of
promise; but he would prefer not to be laughed
at. Come, come, Gerty, get rid of all this
nonsense. Tell him frankly the position; and
don't come bothering me with pretended wrongs
and injuries."

"Do you think I ought to tell him?" said
she, slowly.

"Certainly."

She went away and wrote to Macleod; but
she did not wholly explain her position. She
only begged once more for time to consider
her own feelings. It would be better that he
should not come just now to London. And if
she were convinced, after honest and earnest
questioning of herself, that she had not the
courage and strength of mind necessary for the
great change in her life she had proposed, would

it not be better for his happiness and hers that
the confession should be made ?

Macleod did not answer that letter ; and she
grew alarmed. Several days elapsed. One
afternoon, coming home from rehearsal, she
saw a card lying on the tray on the hall-table.

"Papa," said she, with her face somewhat
paler than usual, " Sir Keith Macleod is in
London ! "

CHAPTER VIII.

A CLIMAX.

She was alone in the drawing-room. She heard the bell ring, and the sound of some one being let in by the front door. Then there was a man's step in the passage outside. The craven heart grew still with dread.

But it was with a great gentleness that he came forward to her, and took both of her trembling hands, and said—

"Gerty, you do not think that I have come to be angry with you—not that!"

He could not but see with those anxious, pained, tender eyes of his that she was very pale; and her heart was now beating so fast —after the first shock of fright—that for a second or two she could not answer him. She withdrew her hands. And all this time he was regarding her face with an eager, wistful intensity.

"It is—so strange—for me to see you again," said he, almost in a bewildered way. "The days have been very long without you—I had almost forgotten what you were like—and now—and now—oh, Gerty, you are not angry with me for troubling you!"

She withdrew a step, and sat down.

"There is a chair," said she: he did not seem to understand what she meant. He was trying to read her thoughts in her eyes, in her manner, in the pale face; and his earnest gaze did not leave her for a moment.

"I know you must be greatly troubled and worried, Gerty; and—and I tried not to come; but your last letter was like the end of the world for me. I thought everything might go then. But then I said, 'Are you a man, and to be cast down by that? She is bewildered by some passing doubt; her mind is sick for the moment; you must go to her, and recall her, and awake her to herself; and you will see her laugh again!' And so I am here, Gerty; and if I am troubling you at a bad time—well, it is only for a moment or two; and you will not mind that? You and I are so different, Gerty! You are all-perfect. You do not want the sympathy of any one. You are satisfied with your own thinkings; you are a world to yourself. But I cannot live without being in sympathy with you. It is a craving—it is like a fire—Well, I did not come here to talk about myself."

"I am sorry you took so much trouble," she said, in a low voice—and there was a nervous restraint in her manner. "You might have answered my letter instead."

"Your letter!" he exclaimed. "Why, Gerty, I could not talk to the letter. It was not yourself. It was no more part of yourself than a glove. You will forget that letter—and all the letters that ever you wrote—let them go away like the leaves of former autumns that are quite forgotten; and instead of the letters, be yourself—as I see you now—proud-spirited and noble—my beautiful Gerty—my wife!"

He made a step forward; and caught her

hand.   She did not see that there were
sudden tears in the imploring eyes.   She only
knew that this vehemence seemed to suffocate
her.

"Keith," said she, and she gently disengaged
her hand, "will you sit down—and we can talk
over this matter calmly, if you please—but I
think it would have been better if you left
us both to explain ourselves in writing.   It
is difficult to say certain things without giving
pain—and you know I don't wish to do that—"

"I know," said he, with an absent look on
his face; and he took the chair she had in-
dicated, and sat down beside her; and now
he was no longer regarding her eyes.

"It is quite true that you and I are different,"
said she, with a certain resolution in her tone,
as if she was determined to get through with
a painful task—"very seriously different in
everything, in our natures, and habits, and
opinions, and all the rest of it.   How we
ever became acquainted I don't know; I am
afraid it was not a fortunate accident for either
of us.   Well——"

Here she stopped. She had not prepared any speech; and she suddenly found herself without a word to say, when words, words, words were all she eagerly wanted in order to cover her retreat. And as for him, he gave her no help. He sat silent—his eyes downcast—a tired and haggard look on his face.

"Well," she resumed, with a violent effort, "I was saying, perhaps we made a mistake in our estimates of each other. That is a very common thing; and sometimes people find out in time, and sometimes they don't. I am sure you agree with me, Keith?"

"Oh yes, Gerty," he answered, absently.

"And then—and then—I am quite ready to confess that I may have been mistaken about myself; and I am afraid you encouraged the mistake. You know, I am quite sure I am not the heroic person you tried to make me believe I was. I have found myself out, Keith; and just in time before making a terrible blunder. I am very glad that it is myself I have to blame. I have got very little resolution. 'Unstable as water'—that is the phrase: perhaps I should

L 2

not like other people to apply it to me; but
I am quite ready to apply it to myself; for I
know it to be true; and it would be a great
pity if any one's life were made miserable
through my fault. Of course, I thought for
a time that I was a very courageous and reso-
lute person—you flattered me into believing it; ·
but I have found myself out since. Don't you
understand, Keith?"

He gave a sign of assent; his silence was
more embarrassing than any protest or any
appeal.

"Oh, I could choose such a wife for you,
Keith—a wife worthy of you—a woman as
womanly as you are manly; and I can think
of her being proud to be your wife, and how
all the people who came to your house would
admire her and love her——"

He looked up in a bewildered way.

"Gerty," he said, "I don't quite know what
it is you are speaking about. You are speaking
as if some strange thing had come between us;
and I was to go one way, and you another,
through all the years to come. Why, that is

all nonsense! See! I can take your hand—
that is the hand that gave me the red rose.
You said you loved me, then; you cannot
have changed already! I have not changed.
What is there that would try to separate us?
Only words, Gerty!—a cloud of words, humming
round the ears and confusing one. Oh, I have
grown heart-sick of them in your letters, Gerty;
until I put the letters away altogether, and I
said, 'They are no more than the leaves of
last autumn: when I see Gerty, and take her
hand, all the words will disappear then.' Your
hand is not made of words, Gerty: it is warm,
and kind, and gentle—it is a woman's hand.
Do you think words are able to make me let
go my grasp of it? I put them away. I do
not hear any more of them. I only know that
you are beside me, Gerty; and I hold your
hand!"

He was now no longer the imploring lover:
there was a strange elation—a sort of triumph
—in his tone.

"Why, Gerty, do you know why I have
come to London? It is to carry you off—not

with the pipes yelling to drown your screams,
as Flora Macdonald's mother was carried off
by her lover—but taking you by the hand,
and waiting for the smile on your face. That
is the way out of all our troubles, Gerty: we
shall be plagued with no more words then. Oh,
I understand it all, sweetheart—your doubts of
yourself, and your thinking about the stage:
it is all a return of the old and evil influences
that you and I thought had been shaken off
for ever. Perhaps that was a little mistake;
but no matter. You will shake them off now,
Gerty. You will show yourself to have the
courage of a woman. It is but one step—and
you are free! Gerty," said he, with a smile on
his face, " do you know what that is ? "

He took from his pocket a printed document,
and opened it. Certain words there that caught
her eye caused her to turn even paler than she
had been; and she would not even touch the
paper. He put it back.

" Are you frightened, sweetheart ? No ! You
will take this one step, and you will see how
all those fancies and doubts will disappear for

ever! Oh, Gerty, when I got this paper into
my pocket to-day, and came out into the street,
I was laughing to myself; and a poor woman
said, 'You are very merry, sir; will you give
a poor old woman a copper?' 'Well,' I said,
'here is a sovereign for you, and perhaps you
will be merry too!'—and I would have given
every one a sovereign if I had had it to give.
But do you know what I was laughing at?—I
was laughing to think what Captain Macallum
would do when you went on board as my wife.
For he put up the flags for you when you were
only a visitor coming to Dare; but when I take
you by the hand, Gerty, as you are going along
the gangway, and when we get on to the paddle-
box, and Captain Macallum comes forward, and
when I tell him that you are now my wife, why
he will not know what to do to welcome you!
And Hamish, too—I think Hamish will go mad
that day. And then, sweetheart, you will go along
to Erraidh, and you will go up to the signal-
house on the rocks, and we will fire a cannon
to tell the men at Dubh-Artach to look out.
And what will be the message you will signal

to them, Gerty, with the great white boards?
Will you send them your compliments, which is
the English way? Ah, but I know what they
will answer to you! They will answer in the
Gaelic; and this will be the answer that will
come to you from the lighthouse—'*A hundred
thousand welcomes to the young bride!*' And
you will soon learn the Gaelic too; and you
will get used to our rough ways; and you will
no longer have any fear of the sea. Some day
you will get so used to us that you will think
the very sea-birds to be your friends, and that
they know when you are going away and when
you are coming back, and that they know you
will not allow any one to shoot them or steal
their eggs in the spring-time. But if you would
rather not have our rough ways, Gerty, I will
go with you wherever you please—did I not
say that to you, sweetheart? There are many
fine houses in Essex—I saw them when I went
down to Woodford with Major Stewart. And
for your sake I would give up the sea altogether;
and I would think no more about boats; and I
would go to Essex with you if I was never to

see one of the sea-birds again. That is what
I will do for your sake, Gerty, if you wish—
though I thought you would be kind to the
poor people around us at Dare, and be proud of
their love for you, and get used to our homely
ways. But I will go into Essex, if you like,
Gerty—so that the sea shall not frighten you;
and you will never be asked to go into one of
our rough boats any more. It shall be just
as you wish, Gerty; whether you want to go
away into Essex, or whether you will come away
with me to the north, that I will say to Captain
Macallum, 'Captain Macallum, what will you
do now that the English lady has been brave
enough to leave her home and her friends to
live with us; and what are we to do now to
show that we are proud and glad of her
coming?'"

Well, tears did gather in her eyes as she
listened to this wild, despairing cry, and her
hands were working nervously with a book
she had taken from the table; but what
answer could she make? In self-defence against
this vehemence she adopted an injured air.

"Really, Keith," said she, in a low voice, "you do not seem to pay any attention to anything I say or write. Surely I have prepared you to understand that my consent to what you propose is quite impossible — for the present, at least. I asked for time to consider."

"I know—I know," said he. "You would wait, and let those doubts close in upon you. But here is a way to defeat them all. Sweetheart, why do you not rise—and give me your hand—and say 'Yes'? There would be no more doubts at all!"

"But surely, Keith, you must understand me when I say that rushing into a marriage in this mad way is a very dangerous thing. You won't look or listen to anything I suggest. And really—well, I think you should have some little consideration for me——"

He regarded her for a moment—with a look almost of wonder; and then he said, hastily—

"Perhaps you are right, Gerty; I should not have been so selfish. But—but you

cannot tell how I have suffered—all through
the night-time thinking and thinking—and
saying to myself that surely you could not
be going away from me—and in the morning, oh! the emptiness of all the sea and the
sky, and you not there to be asked whether
you would go out to Colonsay, or round to
Loch Scridain, or go to see the rock-pigeons
fly out of the caves. It is not a long time
since you were with us, Gerty; but to me it
seems longer than half-a-dozen of winters; for
in the winter I said to myself, 'Ah, well,
she is now working off the term of her imprisonment in the theatre; and when the
days get long again, and the blue skies come
again, she will use the first of her freedom
to come and see the sea-birds about Dare.'
But this last time, Gerty—well, I had strange
doubts and misgivings; and sometimes I
dreamed in the night-time that you were
going away from me altogether—on board a
ship—and I called to you and you would
not even turn your head. Oh, Gerty, I can
see you now as you were then—your head

turned partly aside; and strangers round you; and the ship was going farther and farther away; and if I jumped into the sea, how could I overtake you? But at least the waves would come over me; and I should have forgetfulness."

"Yes, but you seem to think that my letters to you had no meaning whatever," said she, almost petulantly. "Surely I tried to explain clearly enough what our relative positions were?"

"You had got back to the influence of the theatre, Gerty—I would not believe the things you wrote. I said, 'You will go now and rescue her from herself. She is only a girl; she is timid; she believes the foolish things that are said by the people around her.' And then, do you know, sweetheart," said he, with a sad smile on his face, "I thought if I were to go and get this paper, and suddenly show it to you—well, it is not the old romantic way, but I thought you would frankly say 'Yes!' and have an end of all this pain. Why, Gerty, you have been

many a romantic heroine in the theatre; and
you know they are not long in making up
their minds. And the heroines in our old
songs, too: do you know the song of Lizzie
Lindsay, who 'kilted her coats o' green
satin,' and was off to the Highlands before
any one could interfere with her? That is
the way to put an end to doubts. Gerty,
be a brave woman! Be worthy of yourself!
Sweetheart, have you the courage now to
'kilt your coats o' green satin'? And I
know that in the Highlands you will have
as proud a welcome as ever Lord Ronald
Macdonald gave his bride from the south."

Then the strange smile went away from
his face.

"I am tiring you, Gerty," said he.

"Well, you are very much excited, Keith,"
said she; "and you won't listen to what I
have to say. I think your coming to London
was a mistake. You are giving both of us a
great deal of pain; and, as far as I can see,
to no purpose. We could much better have
arrived at a proper notion of each other's

feelings by writing; and the matter is so
serious as to require consideration. If it is
the business of a heroine to plunge two
people into life-long misery without thinking
twice about it, then I am not a heroine.
Her 'coats o' green satin'!—I should like
to know what was the end of that story.
Now really, dear Keith, you must bear with
me if I say that I have a little more prudence
than you; and I must put a check on your
headstrong wishes. And I know there is no
use in our continuing this conversation: you
are too anxious and eager to mind anything
I say. I will write to you."

"Gerty," said he, slowly, "I know you
are not a selfish or cruel woman; and I do
not think you would willingly pain any one.
But if you came to me and said, 'Answer my
question; for it is a question of life or death
to me,' I should not answer that I would
write a letter to you."

"You may call me selfish if you like," said
she, with some show of temper, "but I tell
you once for all that I cannot bear the fatigue

of interviews such as this, and I think it was
very inconsiderate of you to force it on me.
And as for answering a question, the position
we are in is not to be explained with a 'Yes'
or a 'No'—it is mere romance and folly to
speak of people running away and getting
married; for I suppose that is what you mean.
I will write to you, if you like; and give you
every explanation in my power. But I don't
think we shall arrive at any better understanding by your accusing me of selfishness or cruelty."

"Gerty!"

"And if it comes to that," she continued,
with a flush of angry daring in her face, "perhaps I could bring a similar charge against
you, with some better show of reason."

"That I was ever selfish or cruel as regards
you!" said he, with a vague wonder, as if he
had not heard aright.

"Shall I tell you, then," said she, "as you
seem bent on recriminations? Perhaps you
thought I did not understand?—that I was
too frightened to understand? Oh, I knew
very well!"

"I don't know what you mean," said he, in absolute bewilderment.

"What?—not the night we were caught in the storm in crossing to Iona?—and when I clung to your arm, you shook me off, so that you should be free to strike out for yourself if we were thrown into the water. Oh, I don't blame you! It was only natural. But I think you should be cautious in accusing others of selfishness."

For a moment he stood looking at her, with something like fear in his eyes—fear and horror, and a doubt as to whether this thing was possible; and then came the hopeless cry of a breaking heart—

"Oh, God, Gerty! I thought you loved me —and you believed *that!*"

CHAPTER IX.

DREAMS.

THIS long and terrible night: will it never end? Or will not life itself go out, and let the sufferer have rest? The slow and sleepless hours toil on through the darkness; and there is a ticking of a clock in the hushed room; and this agony of pain still throbbing and throbbing in the breaking heart. And then, as the pale dawn shows grey in the windows, the anguish of despair follows him even into the wan realms of sleep, and there are wild visions rising before the sick brain. Strange visions these are; the confused and seething phantasmagoria of a shattered life; himself regarding himself as another figure, and beginning to pity this poor wretch who is not permitted to die. "Poor wretch—poor wretch!" he says to himself. "Did they use to call you

Macleod; and what is it that has brought you to this?"

*　　　*　　　*　　　*　　　*

See now! He lays his head down on the warm heather, on this beautiful summer day; and the seas are all blue around him; and the sun is shining on the white sands of Iona. Far below, the men are singing "*Fhir a bhata,*" and the sea-birds are softly calling. But suddenly there is a horror in his brain; and the day grows black; for an adder has stung him!—it is *Righinn*—the Princess—the Queen of Snakes. O why does she laugh, and look at him so with that clear, cruel look? He would rather not go into this still house where the lidless-eyed creatures are lying in their awful sleep. Why does she laugh? Is it a matter for laughing that a man should be stung by an adder, and all his life grow black around him? For it is then that they put him in a grave; and she—she stands with her foot on it! There is moonlight around; and the jackdaws are wheeling overhead; our voices sound hollow in these dark ruins. But you can hear this, sweetheart: shall I whisper it to you? *" You are standing on the grave of Macleod."*

*　　*　　*　　*　　*

Lo! the grave opens! Why, Hamish, it was no grave at all, but only the long winter; and now we are looking at a strange thing away in the south, for who ever saw before all the beautiful flags that are fluttering there in the summer wind? O sweetheart!—your hand— give me your small, warm, white hand! See! we will go up the steep path by the rocks; and here is the small white house; and have you never seen so great a telescope before? And is it all a haze of heat over the sea; or can you make out the quivering phantom of the light- house—the small grey thing out at the edge of the world? Look! they are signalling now; they know you are here; come out, quick! to the great white boards; and we will send them over a message—and you will see that they will send back a thousand welcomes to the young bride! Our ways are poor; we have no satin bowers to show you, as the old songs say—but do you know who are coming to wait on you?

The beautiful women out of the old songs are
coming to be your handmaidens—I have asked
them—I saw them in many dreams—I spoke
gently to them—and they are coming. Do you
see them ? There is the bonnie Lizzie Lindsay,
who kilted her coats o' green satin to be off
with young Macdonald ; and Burd Helen—she
will come to you pale and beautiful ; and proud
Lady Maisry that was burned for her true love's
sake ; and Mary Scott of Yarrow that set all
men's hearts aflame. See, they will take you
by the hand. They are the Queen's Maries·
There is no other grandeur at Castle Dare.

*   *   *   *   *

Is this Macleod ? They used to say that
Macleod was a man ! They used to say he had
not much fear of anything. But this is only a
poor trembling boy, a coward trembling at everything, and going away to London with a lie on
his lips. And they know how Torquil Macleod
died, and how Roderick Macleod died, and
Ronald, and Olaus the Fair-haired, and Hector
—but the last of them—this poor wretch—what
will they say of him ? " Oh, he died for the

love of a woman!" She struck him in the
heart; and he could not strike back; for she
was a woman. Ah, but if it was a man now!
They say the Macleods are all become sheep;
and their courage has gone; and if they were
to grasp even a Rose-leaf they could not crush
it. It is dangerous to say that; do not trust
to it. Oh, is it you, you poor fool in the newspaper, who are whirling along behind the boat?
Does the swivel work? Are the sharks after
you? Do you hear them behind you—cleaving
the water? The men of Dubh-Artach will have
a good laugh when we whisk you past. What!
you beg for mercy?—come out, then!—you poor
devil! Here is a tarpaulin for you. Give him
a glass of whisky, John Cameron! But you—
even you—if I were to take you over in the
dark, and the storm came on: you would not
think that I thrust you aside to look after myself? You are a stranger; you are helpless in
boats: do you think I would thrust you aside?
It was not fair—oh, it was not fair: if she
wished to kill my heart, there were other things
to say than that. Why, sweetheart, don't you

know that I got the little English boy out of
the water; and you think I would let you
drown! If we were both drowning, now, do
you know what I should do? I would laugh;
and say, "Sweetheart, sweetheart, if we were
not to be together in life, we are now in death,
and that is enough for me."

* * * * *

What is the slow, sad sound that one hears?
The grave is on the lonely island; there is no
one left on the island now; there is nothing
but the grave. "*Man that is born of a woman
hath but a short time to live, and is full of
misery.*" Oh no, not that! That is all over;
the misery is over; and there is peace. This
is the sound of the sea-birds, and the wind
coming over the seas, and the waves on the
rocks. Oh, is it Donald, in the boat going
back to the land? The people have their heads
bent; it is a Lament the boy is playing. And
how will you play the *Cumhadh na Cloinne*
to-night, Donald?—and what will the mother
say? It is six sons she has to think of now;
and Patrick Mòr had but seven dead when he

wrote the Lament of the Children. Janet, see
to her! Tell her it is no matter now; the
peace has come; the misery is over; there is
only the quiet sound of the waves. But you,
Donald, come here. Put down your pipes;
and listen. Do you remember the English lady
who was here in the summer-time; and your
pipes were too loud for her, and were taken
away? She is coming again. She will try
to put her foot on my grave. But you will
watch for her coming, Donald; and you will
go quickly to Hamish; and Hamish will go
down to the shore, and send her back. You
are only a boy, Donald; she would not heed
you; and the ladies at the Castle are too gentle,
and would give her fair words; but Hamish
is not afraid of her—he will drive her back—
she shall not put her foot on my grave—for
my heart can bear no more pain.

* * * * *

And are you going away—*Rose-leaf—Rose-
leaf*—are you sailing away from me on the
smooth waters to the south? I put out my
hand to you; but you are afraid of the hard

hands of the northern people; and you shrink
from me. Do you think we would harm you,
then, that you tremble so? The savage days
are gone; come—we will show you the beautiful islands in the summer-time; and you will
take high courage, and become yourself a
Macleod; and all the people will be proud to
hear of Fionaghal the Fair Stranger who has
come to make her home among us. Oh, our
hands are gentle enough when it is a Rose-leaf
they have to touch. There was blood on them
in the old days; we have washed it off, now:
see—this beautiful red rose you have given me
is not afraid of rough hands! We have no
beautiful roses to give you, but we will give
you a piece of white heather, and that will
secure to you peace and rest and a happy heart
all your days. You will not touch it, sweetheart? Do not be afraid! There is no adder
in it. But if you were to find, now, a white
adder, would you know what to do with it?
There was a sweetheart in an old song knew
what to do with an adder. Do you know the
song? The young man goes back to his home

and he says to his mother, "O make my bed
soon; For I'm weary, weary hunting, and fain
would lie doon." Why do you turn so pale,
sweetheart? There is the whiteness of a white
adder in your cheeks; and your eyes—there is
Death in your eyes! Donald!—Hamish! help!
help!—her foot is coming near to my grave!—
my heart——!

* * * * *

* * * * *

And so, in a paroxysm of wild terror and pain,
he awoke again, and behold, the ghastly white
daylight was in the room—the cold glare of
a day he would fain have never seen. It was
all in a sort of dream that this haggard-faced
man dressed, and drank a cup of tea, and got
outside into the rain. The rain, and the noise
of the cabs, and the gloom of London skies:
these harsh and commonplace things were easier
to bear than the dreams of the sick brain. And
then, somehow or other, he got his way down
to Aldershot, and sought out Norman Ogilvie.

"Macleod!" Ogilvie cried—startled beyond
measure by his appearance.

"I—I wanted to shake hands with you, Ogilvie, before I go," said this hollow-eyed man, who seemed to have grown old.

Ogilvie hesitated for a second or two; and then he said, vehemently—

"Well, Macleod, I am not a sentimental fellow —but—but—hang it! it is too bad. And again and again I have thought of writing to you, as your friend, just within the last week or so; and then I said to myself that tale-bearing never came to any good. But she won't darken Mrs. Ross's door again—that I know. Mrs. Ross went straight to her the other day. There is no nonsense about that woman. And when she got to understand that the story was true, she let Miss White know that she considered you to be a friend of hers, and that—well, you know how women give hints-——"

"But I don't know what you mean, Ogilvie!" he cried, quite bewildered. "Is it a thing for all the world to know? What story is it—when I knew nothing till yesterday?"

"Well, you know now: I saw by your face a minute ago that she had told you the truth at last," Ogilvie said. "Macleod, don't blame me. When I heard of her being about to be married, I did not believe the story——"

Macleod sprang at him, like a tiger, and caught his arm.

"Her getting married?—to whom?"

"Why, don't you know?" Ogilvie said, with his eyes staring. "Oh, yes, you must know. I see you know! Why, the look in your face when you came into this room——"

"Who is the man, Ogilvie?"—and there was the sudden hate of ten thousand devils in his eyes.

"Why, it's that artist-fellow—Lemuel—you don't mean to say she hasn't told you? It is the common story! Mrs. Ross thought it was only a piece of nonsense—she said they were always making those stories about actresses —but she went to Miss White. And when Miss White could not deny it, Mrs. Ross said there and then they had better let their friendship drop. Macleod, I would have written to you— upon my soul, I would have written to you— but how could I imagine you did not know?

And do you really mean to say she has not told you anything of what has been going on recently — what was well known to everybody ?"

And this young man spoke in a passion, too : Keith Macleod was his friend. But Macleod himself seemed, with some powerful effort of will, to have got the better of his sudden and fierce hate ; he sat down again ; he spoke in a low voice ; but there was a dark look in his eyes.

"No," said he, slowly, "she has not told me all about it. Well, she did tell me about a poor creature—a woman-man—a thing of affectation, with his paint-box and his velvet coat, and his furniture : Ogilvie, have you got any brandy ?"

Ogilvie rang, and got some brandy, some water, a tumbler, and a wine-glass placed on the table. Macleod, with a hand that trembled violently, filled the tumbler half full with brandy.

"And she could not deny the story to Mrs. Ross ?" said he, with a strange and hard smile on his face. "It was her modesty. Ah, you don't know, Ogilvie, what an exalted soul she has. She is full of idealisms. She could not explain all that to Mrs. Ross. *I* know. And when she found herself too weak to carry out her aspirations, she sought help. Is that it? She would gain assurance and courage from the woman-man?"

He pushed the tumbler away; his hand was still trembling violently.

"I will not touch that, Ogilvie," said he, "for I have not much mastery over myself. I am going away now—I am going back now to the Highlands—oh! you do not know what I have become since I met that woman—a coward, and a liar! They wouldn't have you sit down at the mess-table, Ogilvie, if you were that: would they? I dare not stay in London now. I must run away now—like a hare that is hunted. It would not be good for her or for me that I should stay any longer in London."

He rose, and held out his hand: there was a curious glazed look on his eyes. Ogilvie pressed him back into the chair again.

"You are not going out in this condition, Macleod—you don't know what you are doing.

Come now, let us be reasonable; let us talk over
the thing like men. And I must say, first of
all, that I am heartily glad of it for your sake.
It will be a hard twist at first; but bless you!
lots of fellows have had to fight through the
same thing, and they come up smiling after it,
and you would scarcely know the difference.
Don't imagine I am surprised:—oh, no. I
never did believe in that young woman; I
thought she was a deuced sight too clever; and
when she used to go about humbugging this
one and the other with her innocent airs, I said
to myself, 'Oh, it's all very well; but *she* knows
what she is about.' Of course, there was no
use talking to you. I believe at one time Mrs.
Ross was considering whether she ought not
to give you a hint, seeing you had met Miss
White first at her house, that the young lady
was rather clever at flirtation, and that you
ought to keep a sharp look-out. But then you
would only have blazed up in anger. It was
no use talking to you. And then, after all, I
said that if you were so bent on marrying her,
the chances were that you would have no diffi-

culty, for I thought the bribe of her being called
Lady Macleod would be enough for any actress.
As for the man Lemuel, no doubt he is a very
great man, as people say; but I don't know
much about these things myself; and—and—
I think it is very plucky of Mrs. Ross to cut
off two of her lions at one stroke. It shows
she must have taken an uncommon liking for
you. So you must cheer up; Macleod. If women
take a fancy to you like that, you'll easily get
a better wife than Miss White would have made.
Mind you, I don't go back from anything I ever
said of her. She is a handsome woman, and
no mistake; and I will say that she is the best
waltzer that I ever met with in the whole course
of my life—without exception. But she's the
sort of woman who, if I married her, would
want some looking after—I mean, that is my
impression. The fact is, Macleod, away there
in Mull you have been brought up too much on
books and your own imagination. You were
ready to believe any pretty woman, with soft
English ways, an angel. Well, you have had
a twister; but you'll come through it; and you

will get to believe after all that women are
very good creatures, just as men are very
good creatures, when you get the right sort.
Come now, Macleod, pull yourself together.
Perhaps I have just as hard an opinion of her
conduct towards you as you have yourself. But
you know Tommy Moore, or some fellow like
that, says—'If she be not fair to me, what the
devil care I how fair she be?' And if I were
you, I would have a drop of brandy—but not
half a tumbler-full."

But neither Lieutenant Ogilvie's pert com-
mon-sense, nor his apt and accurate quotation,
nor the proffered brandy, seemed to alter
much the mood of this haggard-faced man.
He rose.

"I think I will go now," said he in a low
voice. "You won't take it unkindly, Ogilvie,
that I don't stop to talk with you—it is a
strange story you have told me—I want time
to think over it. Good-bye!"

"The fact is, Macleod," Ogilvie stammered, as
he regarded his friend's face, "I don't like to
leave you. Won't you stay and dine with our

fellows? Or shall I see if I can run up to London with you?"

"No, thank you, Ogilvie," said he. "And have you any message for the mother and Janet?"

"Oh, I hope you will remember me most kindly to them. At least, I will go to the station with you, Macleod."

"Thank you, Ogilvie; but I would rather go alone. Good-bye, now."

He shook hands with his friend—in an absent sort of way—and left. But while yet his hand was on the door, he turned and said—

"Oh, do you remember my gun that has the shot barrel and the rifle barrel?"

"Yes, certainly."

"Would you like to have that, Ogilvie? —we sometimes had it when we were out together."

"Do you think I would take your gun from you, Macleod?" said the other. "You will soon have plenty of use for it now."

"Good-bye, then, Ogilvie," said he, and he

left, and went out into the world of rain and lowering skies and darkening moors.

And when he went back to Dare it was a wet day also ; but he was very cheerful ; and he had a friendly word for all whom he met ; and he told the mother and Janet that he had got home at last, and meant to go no more a-roving. But that evening, after dinner, when Donald began to play the Lament for the memory of the five sons of Dare, Macleod uttered a sort of stifled cry, and there were tears running down his cheeks—which was a strange thing for a man ; and he rose and left the hall, just as a woman would have done. And his mother sate there, cold, and pale, and trembling ; but the gentle cousin Janet called out, with a piteous trouble in her eyes—

"Oh, auntie, have you seen the look on our Keith's face, ever since he came ashore to-day ?"

"I know it, Janet," said she. "I have seen it. That woman has broken his heart—and he is the last of my six brave lads."

' They could not speak any more now; for Donald had come up the hall; and he was playing the wild, sad wail of the *Cumhadh na Cloinne*.

CHAPTER X.

A LAST HOPE.

THOSE sleepless nights of passionate yearning
and despair—those days of sullen gloom broken
only by wild cravings for revenge that went
through his brain like spasms of fire: these
were killing this man. His face grew haggard
and grey; his eyes morose and hopeless; he
shunned people as if he feared their scrutiny;
he brooded over the past in a silence he did
not wish to have broken by any human voice.
This was no longer Macleod of Dare. It was
the wreck of a man — drifting no one knew
whither.

And in those dark and morbid reveries
there was no longer any bewilderment. He
saw clearly how he had been tricked and
played with. He understood now the cold-

ness she had shown on coming to Dare ; her
desire to get away again ; her impatience with
his appeals ; her anxiety that communication between them should be solely by letter. " Yes,
yes," he would say to himself—and sometimes
he would laugh aloud in the solitude of the
hills, " she was prudent. She was a woman
of the world, as Stewart used to say. She
would not quite throw me off—she would not
be quite frank with me—until she had made
sure of the other. And in her trouble of
doubt, when she was trying to be better than
herself, and anxious to have guidance, *that* was
the guide she turned to—the woman-man, the
dabbler in paint-boxes, the critic of carpets
and wall-papers ! "

Sometimes he grew to hate her. She had
destroyed the world for him. She had destroyed his faith in the honesty and honour
of womanhood. She had played with him as
with a toy—a fancy of the brain—and thrown
him aside when something new was presented
to her. And when a man is stung by a white
adder, does he not turn and stamp with his

heel? Is he not bound to crush the creature
out of existence, to keep God's earth and the
free sunlight sweet and pure?

But then—but then—the beauty of her!
In dreams he heard her low, sweet laugh
again; he saw the beautiful brown hair; he
surrendered to the irresistible witchery of the
clear and lovely eyes. What would not a man
give for one last, wild kiss of the laughing
and half-parted lips? His life? And if that
life happened to be a mere broken and useless
thing—a hateful thing—would he not gladly
and proudly fling it away? One long, lingering, despairing kiss; and then a deep draught
of Death's black wine!

One day he was riding down to the fishing-
station when he met John Macintyre the post-
man, who handed him a letter, and passed on.
Macleod opened this letter with some trepidation, for it was from London; but it was in
Norman Ogilvie's handwriting.

"DEAR MACLEOD,—I thought you might
like to hear the latest news. I cut the

enclosed from a sort of half-sporting, half-theatrical paper our fellows get; no doubt the paragraph is true enough. And I wish it was well over and done with; and she married out of hand; for I know until that is so, you will be torturing yourself with all sorts of projects and fancies. Good-bye, old fellow. I suppose when you offered me the gun, you thought your life had collapsed altogether, and that you would have no further use for anything. But no doubt, after the first shock, you have thought better of that. How are the birds? I hear rather bad accounts from Ross; but then he is always complaining about something.

"Yours sincerely,

"NORMAN OGILVIE."

And then he unfolded the newspaper cutting which Ogilvie had enclosed. The paragraph of gossip announced that the Piccadilly Theatre would shortly be closed for repairs; but that the projected provincial tour of the company had been abandoned. On the re-opening of

the theatre, a play, which was now in preparation, written by Mr. Gregory Lemuel,
would be produced. "It is understood," continued the newsman, "that Miss Gertrude
White, the young and gifted actress who has
been the chief attraction at the Piccadilly
Theatre for two years back, is to be married
to Mr. Lionel Lemuel, the well-known artist;
but the public have no reason to fear the with-
drawal of so popular a favourite; for she has
consented to take the chief *rôle* in the new
play, which is said to be of a tragic nature."

Macleod put the letter and its enclosure
into his pocket; and rode on. The hand that
held the bridle shook somewhat; that was all.

He met Hamish.

"Oh, Hamish!" he cried quite gaily.
"Hamish, will you go to the wedding?"

"What wedding, sir?" said the old man;
but well he knew. If there was any one
blind to what had been going on, that was
not Hamish; and again and again he had in
his heart cursed the English traitress who had
destroyed his master's peace.

"Why, do you not remember the English lady that was here not so long ago? And she is going to be married. And would you like to go to the wedding, Hamish?"

He scarcely seemed to know what he was saying in this wild way; there was a strange look in his eyes, though apparently he was very merry. And this was the first word he had uttered about Gertrude White to any living being at Dare ever since his last return from the south.

Now what was Hamish's answer to this gay invitation? The Gaelic tongue has very few of those meaningless expletives which, in other languages, express mere annoyance or temper; when a Highlander swears, he usually swears in English. But the Gaelic curse is a much more solemn and deliberate affair.

"*May her soul dwell in the lowermost hall of perdition!*"—that was the answer that Hamish made; and there was a blaze of anger in the keen eyes and in the proud and handsome face.

"Oh, yes," continued the old man in his native tongue, and he spoke rapidly and passionately,

"I am only a serving-man; and perhaps a serving-man ought not to speak; but perhaps sometimes he will speak. And have I not seen it all, Sir Keith?—and no more of the pink letters coming; and you going about a changed man, as if there was nothing more in life for you? And now you ask me if I will go to the wedding! And what do I say to you, Sir Keith? I say this to you—that the woman is not now living who will put that shame on Macleod of Dare!"

Macleod regarded the old man's angry vehemence almost indifferently; he had grown to pay little heed to anything around him.

"Oh, yes, it is a fine thing for the English lady," said Hamish, with the same proud fierceness, "to come here and amuse herself. But she does not know the Mull men yet. Do you think, Sir Keith, that any one of your forefathers would have had this shame put upon him? I think not. I think he would have said, 'Come, lads, here is a proud madam that does not know that a man's will is stronger than a woman's will; and we will teach her a lesson. And before she has learned that lesson, she will discover that it is not safe to trifle with a Macleod of Dare.'   And you ask me if I will go to the wedding !   I have known you since you were a child, Sir Keith ; and I put the first gun in your hand ; and I saw you catch your first salmon : it is not right to laugh at an old man."

"Laughing at you, Hamish ?   I gave you an invitation to a wedding ! "

"And if I was going to that wedding," said Hamish, with a return of that fierce light to the grey eyes, " do you know how I would go to the wedding ?   I would take two or three of the young lads with me.   We would make a fine party for the wedding.   Oh, yes ; a fine party ! And if the English church is a fine church, can we not take off our caps as well as any one ? But when the pretty madam came in, I would say to myself, 'O yes, my fine madam, you forgot it was a Macleod you had to deal with, and not a child, and you did not think you would have a visit from two or three of the Mull lads ? "

"And what then ? " Macleod said with a smile

—though this picture of his sweetheart coming into the church as the bride of another man had paled his cheek.

"And before she had brought that shame on the house of Dare," said Hamish, excitedly, "do you not think that I would seize her—that I would seize her with my own hands? And when the young lads and I had thrust her down into the cabin of the yacht—oh, yes, when we had thrust her down and shut the companion, do you think the proud madam would be quite so proud?"

Macleod laughed a loud laugh.

"Why, Hamish, you want to become a famous person! You would carry off a popular actress; and have all the country ringing with the exploit! And would you have a piper, too, to drown her screams—just as Macdonald of Armadale did when he came with his men to South Uist and carried off Flora Macdonald's mother?"

"And was there ever a better marriage than that—as I have heard many a man of Skye say?" Hamish exclaimed, eagerly. "Oh yes, it is good for a woman to know that a man's will is stronger than a woman's will! And when we have the

fine English madam caged up in the cabin, and
we are coming away to the north again, she will
not have so many fine airs, I think. And if the
will cannot be broken, it is the neck that can be
broken; and better that than that Sir Keith
Macleod should have a shame put on him."

"Hamish, Hamish, how will you dare to go
into the church at Salen next Sunday?" Mac-
cleod said; but he was now regarding the old
man with a strange curiosity.

"Men were made before churches were
thought of," Hamish said, curtly; and then
Macleod laughed, and rode on.

The laugh soon died away from his face. Here
was the stone bridge on which she used to lean
to drop pebbles into the whirling clear water.
Was there not some impression even yet of her
soft warm arm on the velvet moss? And what
had the voice of the streamlet told him in the
days long ago—that the summer time was made
for happy lovers; that she was coming; that he
should take her hand and show her the beautiful
islands and the sunlit seas before the darkening
skies of the winter came over them. And here

was the summer sea; and moist, warm odours
were in the larch-wood; and out there Ulva was
shining green, and there was sunlight on the
islands and on the rocks of Erisgeir. But she
—where was she? Perhaps standing before a
mirror; with a dress all of white; and trying how
orange-blossoms would best lie in her soft brown
hair. · Her arms are uplifted to her head; she
smiles:—could not one suddenly seize her now by
the waist, and bear her off, with the smile changed
to a blanched look of fear? The wild pirates
have got her; the Rose-leaf is crushed in the
cruel northern hands; at last—at last—what is
in the scabbard has been drawn, and declared,
and she screams in her terror!

Then he fell to brooding again over Hamish's
mad scheme. The fine English church of
Hamish's imagination was no doubt a little
stone building that a handful of sailors could
carry at a rush. And of course the yacht must
needs be close by; for there was no land in
Hamish's mind that was out of sight of the salt
water. And what consideration would this old
man have for delicate fancies and studies in

moral science? The fine madam had been chosen to be the bride of Macleod of Dare; that was enough. If her will would not bend, it would have to be broken. That was the good old way : was there ever a happier wife than the Lady of Armadale, who had been carried screaming down stairs in the night time, and placed in her lover's boat, with the pipes playing a wild pibroch all the time?

Macleod was in the library that night when Hamish came to him with some papers. And just as the old man was about to leave, Macleod said to him—

" Well, that was a pretty story you told me this morning, Hamish, about the carrying off of the young English lady. And have you thought any more about it?"

" I have thought enough about it," Hamish said, in his native tongue.

" Then perhaps you could tell me, when you start on this fine expedition, how you are going to have the yacht taken to London? The lads of Mull are very clever, Hamish, I know; but do you think than any one of them can steer the

Umpire all the way from Loch-na-Keal to the river Thames?"

"Is it the river Thames?" said Hamish, with superb contempt. "And is that all—the river Thames? Do you know this, Sir Keith, that my cousin Colin Laing, that has a whisky-shop now in Greenock, has been all over the world, and at China and other places; and he was the mate of many a big vessel; and do you think he could not take the *Umpire* from Loch-na-Keal to London? And I would only have to send a line to him and say, 'Colin, it is Sir Keith Macleod himself that will want you to do this;' and then he will leave twenty or thirty shops, ay, fifty and a hundred shops, and think no more of them at all. Oh, yes, it is very true what you say, Sir Keith. There is no one knows better than I the soundings in Loch Scridain and Loch Tua; and you have said yourself that there is not a bank or a rock about the islands that I do not know; but I have not been to London. No, I have not been to London. But is there any great trouble in getting to London? No, none at all; when we have Colin Laing on board."

Macleod was apparently making a gay joke of the matter; but there was an anxious, intense look in his eyes all the same—even when he was staring absently at the table before him.

"Oh, yes, Hamish," he said, laughing in a constrained manner, "that would be a fine story to tell. And you would become very famous— just as if you were working for fame in a theatre; and all the people would be talking about you. And when you got to London, how would you get through the London streets?"

"It is my cousin who would show me the way: has he not been to London more times than I have been to Stornoway?"

"But the streets of London—they would cover all the ground between here and Loch-na-Keal; and how would you carry the young lady through them?"

"We would carry her," said Hamish, curtly.

"With the bagpipes to drown her screams?"

"I would drown her screams myself," said Hamish, with a sudden savageness; and he added something that Macleod did not hear.

"Do you know that I am a magistrate,
Hamish?"

"I know it, Sir Keith."

"And when you come to me with this pro-
posal, do you know what I should do?"

"I know what the old Macleods of Dare
would have done," said Hamish, proudly,
"before they let this shame come on them.
And you, Sir Keith—you are a Macleod too;
ay, and the bravest lad that ever was born in
Castle Dare! And you will not suffer this
thing any longer, Sir Keith; for it is a sore
heart I have from the morning till night; and
it is only a serving-man that I am; but sometimes when I will see you going about—and
nothing now cared for, but a great trouble on
your face—oh, then I say to myself, 'Hamish,
you are an old man, and you have not long
to live; but before you die you will teach the
fine English madam what it is to bring a
shame on Sir Keith Macleod!'"

"Ah, well, good-night now, Hamish: I am
tired," he said; and the old man slowly left.

He was tired—if one might judge by the

haggard cheeks and the heavy eyes; but he did not go to sleep. He did not even go to bed. He spent the live-long night, as he had spent too many lately, in nervously pacing to and fro within this hushed chamber; or seated with his arms on the table, and the aching head resting on his clasped hands. And again those wild visions came to torture him—the product of a sick heart and a bewildered brain; only now there was a new element introduced. This mad project of Hamish's, at which he would have laughed in a saner mood, began to intertwist itself with all these passionate longings and these troubled dreams of what might yet be possible to him on earth; and wherever he turned it was suggested to him; and whatever was the craving and desire of the moment, this, and only this, was the way to reach it. For if one were mad with pain; and determined to crush the white adder that had stung one, what better way than to seize the hateful thing and cage it, so that it should do no more harm among the sons of men? Or if one were mad because of the love of a beautiful Princess—and she far away, and dressed in bridal robes: what better way than to take her hand, and say, "Quick, quick, to the shore! For the summer seas are waiting for you; and there is a home for the bride far away in the north"? Or if it was only one wild, despairing effort—one last means of trying—to bring her heart back again? Or if there was but the one fierce, captured kiss of those lips no longer laughing at all? Men had ventured more for far less reward, surely! And what remained to him in life but this? There was at least the splendid joy of daring and action!

The hours passed; and sometimes he fell into a troubled sleep as he sat with his head bent on his hands—but then it was only to see those beautiful pictures of her that made his heart ache all the more. And sometimes he saw her in sailor-like white and blue, as she was stepping down from the steamer; and sometimes he saw the merry Duchess coming forward through the ballroom, with her saucy eyes and her laughing and parted lips; and sometimes he saw her before a mirror; and again she smiled—but his heart would fain have cried aloud in its anguish. Then again he would start up, and look at the window. Was he impatient for the day?

The lamp still burned in the hushed chamber. With trembling fingers he took out the letter Ogilvie had written to him, and held the slip of printed paper before his bewildered gaze. "The young and gifted actress." She is "shortly to be married." And the new piece that all the world will come to see, as soon as she is returned from the wedding tour, is "of a tragic nature."

* * * * *

Hamish, Hamish, do you hear these things? Do you know what they mean? Oh, we will have to look sharp if we are to be there ir time. Come along, you brave lads; it is not the first time a Macleod has carried off a bride. And will she cry, do you think?—for we have no pipes to drown her screams. Ah, but we will manage it another way than that, Hamish! You have no cunning, you old man! There will be no scream, when the white adder is seized and caged.

* * * * *

But surely no white adder! O sweetheart, you
gave me a red rose! And do you remember the
night in the garden, with the moonlight around
us, and the favour you wore next your heart was
the badge of the Macleods? You were not afraid
of the Macleods then; you had no fear of the
rude northern people; you said they would not
crush a pale Rose-leaf. And now—now—see! I
have rescued you; and those people will per-
suade you no longer; I have taken you away—
you are free! And will you come up on deck,
now; and look around on the summer sea? And
shall we put into some port, and telegraph that
the runaway bride is happy enough; and that
they will hear of her next from Castle Dare?
Look around, sweetheart; surely you know the
old boat. And here is Christina to wait on you;
and Hamish—Hamish will curse you no more—
he will be your friend now. Oh, you make the
mother's heart glad at last: she has not smiled
for many a day.

  *   *   *   *   *

Or is it the proud madam that is below,
Hamish; and she will not speak; and she sits

alone in all her finery? And what are we to do
with her now, then—to break her will? Do
you think she will speak when she is in the
midst of the silence of the northern seas? Or
will they be after us, Hamish? Oh, that would
be a fine chase, indeed; and we would lead them
a fine dance through the Western Isles; and I
think you would try their knowledge of the
channels and the banks. And the painter-fellow,
Hamish, the woman-man, the dabbler—would he
be in the boat behind us?—or would he be down
below, in bed in the cabin, with a nurse to attend
him? Come along, then!—but beware of the
overfalls off Tiree, you southern men! Or is it a
race for Barra Head; and who will be at Vater-
say first? There is good fishing-ground on the
Sgriobh bhan, Hamish; they may as well stop to
fish as seek to catch us among our western
isles! See, the dark is coming down; is that the
Monach-light in the north?—Hamish, Hamish,
we are on the rocks!—and there is no one to
help her! Oh, sweetheart!—sweetheart!—

    *   *   *   *   *

The brief fit of struggling sleep is over; he

rises, and goes to the window; and now, if he is
impatient for the new day, behold! the new day
is here.   Oh, see, how the wan light of the morning meets the wan face!   It is the face of a man
who has been close to Death; it is the face of a
man who is desperate.   And if, after the terrible
battle of the night, with its uncontrollable
yearning and its unbearable pain, the fierce and
bitter resolve is taken?—if there remains but
this one last despairing venture for all that made
life worth having?   How wildly the drowning
man clutches at this or that, so only that he may
breathe for yet a moment more.   He knows not
what miracle may save him; he knows not where
there is any land; but only to live—only to
breathe for another moment—that is his cry.
And then, mayhap, amid the wild whirl of waves,
if he were suddenly to catch sight of the shore;
and think that he was getting near to that; and
see awaiting him there a white Princess, with a
smile on her lips, and a red rose in her outstretched hand?   Would he not make one last
convulsive effort before the black waters dragged
him down?

CHAPTER XI.

THE WHITE-WINGED DOVE.

THE mere thought of this action, swift, imme-
diate, impetuous, seemed to give relief to the
burning brain. He went outside, and walked
down to the shore; all the world was asleep;
but the day had broken fair and pleasant, and
the sea was calm and blue. Was not that a
good omen? After all, then, there was still the
wild, glad hope that Fionaghal might come and
live in her northern home; the summer days
had not gone for ever; they might still find a
red rose for her bosom at Castle Dare.

And then he tried to deceive himself. Was
not this a mere lover's stratagem? Was not all
fair in love as in war? Surely she would forgive
him, for the sake of the great love he bore her,
and the happiness he would try to bring her all

the rest of her life? And no sailor, he would take care, would lay his rough hand on her gentle arm. That was the folly of Hamish. There was no chance in these days for a band of northern pirates to rush into a church and carry off a screaming bride. There were other ways than that; gentler ways; and the victim of the conspiracy, why, she would only laugh in the happy after-time and be glad that he had succeeded. And meanwhile, he rejoiced that so much had to be done. Oh yes, there was plenty to think about now, other than those terrible visions of the night. There was work to do; and the cold sea-air was cooling the fevered brain, so that it all seemed pleasant and easy and glad. There was Colin Laing to be summoned from Greenock, and questioned. The yacht had to be provisioned for a long voyage. He had to prepare the mother and Janet for his going away. And might not Norman Ogilvie find out somehow when the marriage was to be, so that he would know how much time was left him?

But with all this eagerness and haste, he kept

whispering to himself counsels of caution and
prudence. He dared not awaken her suspicion
by professing too much forgiveness or friendliness. He wrote to her—with what a trembling
hand he put down those words, *Dear Gertrude,*
on paper, and how wistfully he regarded them!
—but the letter was a proud and cold letter.
He said that he had been informed she was
about to be married; he wished to ascertain
from herself whether that was true. He would
not reproach her, either with treachery or deceit;
if this was true, passionate words would not be
of much avail. But he would prefer to be
assured, one way or another, by her own hand.
That was the substance of the letter.

And then the answer! He almost feared she
would not write. But when Hamish himself
brought that pink envelope to him, how his
heart beat! And the old man stood there in
silence, and with gloom on his face : was there
to be, after all, no act of vengeance on her who
had betrayed Macleod of Dare?

The few words seemed to have been written
with unsteady fingers. He read them again and

again. Surely there was no dark mystery within them?—

"*Dear Keith, I cannot bear to write to you. I do not know how it has all happened. Forgive me if you can; and forget me. G.*"

"Oh, Hamish," said he, with a strange laugh, "is it an easy thing to forget that you have been alive? That would be an easy thing, if one were to ask you? But is not Colin Laing coming here to-day?"

"Oh yes, Sir Keith," Hamish said, with his eyes lighting up eagerly, " he will be here with the *Pioneer*, and I will send the boat out for him. Oh, yes, and you are wanting to see him, Sir Keith?"

"Why, of course!" Macleod said. " If we are going away on a long voyage, do we not want a good pilot?"

"And we are going, Sir Keith?" the old man said; and there was a look of proud triumph in the keen face.

"Oh, I do not know yet," Macleod said, impatiently. "But you will tell Christina that, if we are going away to the south, we may have lady-visitors come on board, some day or another; and she would be better than a young lass to look after them, and make them comfortable on board. And if there are any clothes or ribbons she may want from Salen, Donald can go over with the pony : and you will not spare any money, Hamish."

" Very well, sir."

" And you will not send the boat out to the *Pioneer* till I give you a letter; and you will ask the clerk to be so kind as to post it for me to-night at Oban ; he must not forget that."

" Very well, sir," said Hamish ; and he left the room, with a determined look about his lips, but with a glad light in his eyes.

This was the second letter that Macleod wrote; and he had to keep whispering to himself " Caution ! caution ! " or he would have broken into some wild appeal to his sweetheart far away.

" DEAR GERTRUDE," he wrote, " I gather from your note that it is true you are going to be married. I had heard some time ago ; so your letter was no great shock to me; and what I have suffered—well, that can be of no interest to you now, and it will do me no good to recall it. As to your message, I would forgive you freely; but how can I forget? Can you forget? Do you remember the red rose? But that is all over now, I suppose; and I should not wonder if I were after all to be able to obey you, and to forget very thoroughly—not that alone, but everything else. For I have been rather ill of late—more through sleeplessness than any other cause, I think; and they say I must go for a long sea-voyage; and the mother and Janet both say I should be more at home in the old *Umpire*—with Hamish and Christina, and my own people round me—than in a steamer; and so I may not hear of you again until you are separated from me for ever. But I write now to ask you if you would like your letters returned; and one or two keepsakes; and the photographs: I would not like them to fall into other hands; and sometimes I feel so sick at heart that I doubt whether I shall ever again get back to Dare. There are some flowers, too;

but I would ask to be allowed to keep them, if
you have no objection—and the sketch of Ulva,
that you made on the deck of the *Umpire*, when
we were coming back from Iona, I would like
to keep that, if you have no objection. And
I remain your faithful friend,

"KEITH MACLEOD."

Now at the moment he was writing this letter,
Lady Macleod and her niece were together; the
old lady at her spinning-wheel, the younger one
sewing. And Janet Macleod was saying—

"Oh, auntie, I am so glad Keith is going
away now in the yacht; and you must not be
vexed at all or troubled if he stays a long time;
for what else can make him well again? Why,
you know that he has not been Keith at all of
late—he is quite another man—I do not think
any one would recognise him. And surely there
can be no better cure for sleeplessness than the
rough work of the yachting; and you know
Keith will take his share, in despite of Hamish;
and if he goes away to the south, they will have
watches, and he will take his watch with the

others, and his turn at the helm. Oh, you will see the change when he comes back to us!"

The old lady's eyes had slowly filled with tears.

"And do you think it is sleeplessness, Janet," said she, "that is the matter with our Keith? Ah, but you know better than that, Janet."

Janet Macleod's face grew suddenly red; but she said, hastily—

"Why, auntie, have I not heard him walking up and down all the night, whether it was in his room or in the library? And then he is out before any one is up: oh, yes, I know that when you cannot sleep, the face grows white, and the eyes grow tired. And he has not been himself at all—going away like that from every one; and having nothing to say; and going away by himself over the moors. The night before last, when he came back from Kinloch, he was wet through, and he only lay down on the bed, as Hamish told me, and would have slept there all the night, but for Hamish. And do you not think that was to get sleep at last— that he had been walking so far, and coming through the shallows of Loch Scridain too?

Ah, but you will see the difference, auntie, when he comes back on board the *Umpire*, and we will go down to the shore; and we will be glad to see him that day."

"Oh yes, Janet," the old lady said, and the tears were running down her face, "but you know—you know. And if he had married you, Janet, and stayed at home at Dare, there would have been none of all this trouble. And now —what is there now? It is the young English lady that has broken his heart; and he is no longer a son to me, and he is no longer your cousin, Janet; but a broken-hearted man, that does not care for anything. You are very kind, Janet; you would not say any harm of any one. But I am his mother—I—I—well, if the woman was to come here this day, do you think I would not speak? It was a bad day for us all that he went away—instead of marrying you, Janet."

"But you know that could never have been, auntie," said the gentle-eyed cousin, though there was some conscious flush of pride in her cheeks. "I could never have married Keith."

"But why, Janet?'

"You have no right to ask me, auntie. But he and I—we did not care for each other—I mean, we never could have been married. I hope you will not speak about that any more, auntie."

"And some day they will take me, too, away from Dare," said the old dame, and the spinning-wheel was left unheeded, "and I cannot go into the grave with my five brave lads—for where are they all now, Janet?—in Arizona one, in Africa one, and two in the Crimea, and my brave Hector at Königgrätz. But that is not much; I shall be meeting them all together; and do you not think I shall be glad to see them all together again just as it was in the old days; and they will come to meet me; and they will be glad enough to have the mother with them once again? But, Janet, Janet, how can I go to them? What will I say to them when they ask about Keith—about Keith, my Benjamin, my youngest, my hand-some lad?"

The old woman was sobbing bitterly; and

Janet went to her and put her arms round her, and said,—

"Why, auntie, you must not think of such things. You will send Keith away in low spirits if you have not a bright face and a smile for him when he goes away."

"But you do not know—you do not know," the old woman said, "what Keith has done for me. The others—oh, yes they were brave lads ; and very proud of their name, too ; and they would not disgrace their name wherever they went ; and if they died—that is nothing ; for they will be together again now : and what harm is there ? But Keith, he was the one that did more than any of them ; for he stayed at home for my sake ; and when other people were talking about this regiment and that regiment, Keith would not tell me what was sore at his heart ; and never once did he say, 'Mother, I must go away like the rest,' though it was in his blood to go away. And what have I done now ?—and what am I to say to his brothers when they come to ask me ? I will say to them, 'Oh, yes, he was the hand-

somest of all my six lads; and he had the
proudest heart, too; but, I kept him at home.
And what came of it all? Would it not be
better now that he was lying buried in the
jungle of the Gold Coast, or at Königgrätz, or
in the Crimea?"

"Oh, surely not, auntie! Keith will come
back to us soon; and when you see him well
and strong again; and when you hear his laugh
about the house—surely you will not be wishing that he was in his grave? Why, what is
the matter with you to-day, auntie?"

"The others did not suffer much, Janet; and
to three of them, any way, it was only a bullet
—a cry—and then the death-sleep of a brave
man, and the grave of a Macleod. But Keith,
Janet—he is my youngest—he is nearer to
my heart than any of them: do you not see
his face?"

"Yes, auntie," Janet Macleod said, in a low
voice. "But he will get over that. He will
come back to us strong and well."

"Oh, yes, he will come back to us strong and
well!" said the old lady, almost wildly, and she

rose, and her face was pale. "But I think it is a good thing for that woman that my other sons are all away now; for they had quick tempers, those lads; and they would not like to see their brother murdered."

"Murdered, auntie!"

Lady Macleod would have answered in the same wild passionate way; but at this very moment her son entered. She turned quickly; she almost feared to meet the look of his haggard face. But Keith Macleod said, quite cheerfully—

"Well now, Janet, will you go round to-day to look at the *Umpire?* And will you come too, mother? Oh, she is made very smart now; just as if we were all going away to see the Queen."

"I cannot go to-day, Keith," said his mother, and she left the room before he had time to notice that she was strangely excited.

"I think I will go some other day, Keith," his cousin said, gently, "just before you start, that I may be sure you have not forgotten anything. And, of course, you will take the ladies' cabin, Keith, for yourself; for there is more light in that; and it is further away from the noise of the forecastle in the morning. But how can you be going to-day, Keith, when the man from Greenock will be here soon now?"

"Why, I forgot that, Janet," said he laughing in a nervous way. "I forgot that, though I was talking to Hamish about him only a little while ago. And I think I might as well go out to meet the *Pioneer* myself, if the boat has not left yet. Is there anything you would like to get from Oban, Janet?"

"No, nothing, thank you, Keith," said she; and then he left; and he was in time to get into the big sailing-boat before it went out to meet the steamer.

This cousin of Hamish, who jumped into the boat when Macleod's letter had been handed up to the clerk, was a little, black-haired Celt, beady-eyed, nervous, but with the affectation of a sailor's bluffness, and he wore rings in his ears. However, when he was got ashore, and taken into the library, Macleod very speedily found

out that the man had some fair skill in navi-
gation, and that he had certainly been into a
good number of ports in his lifetime. And if
one were taking the *Umpire* into the mouth
of the Thames, now? Mr. Laing looked doubt-
fully at the general chart Macleod had; he
said he would rather have a special chart which
he could get at Greenock; for there were a
great many banks about the mouth of the
Thames; and he was not sure that he could
remember the channel. And if one wished to
go further up the river, to some anchorage in
communication by rail with London? Oh, yes,
there was Erith. And if one would rather have
moorings than an anchorage, so that one might
slip away without trouble when the tide and
wind were favourable? Oh, yes, there was
nothing simpler than that. There were many
yachts about Erith; and surely the pier-master
could get the *Umpire* the loan of moorings.
All through Castle Dare it was understood that
there was no distinct destination marked down
for the *Umpire* on this suddenly-arranged
voyage of hers; but all the same Sir Keith

Macleod's inquiries went no further, at present at least, than the river Thames.

There came another letter, in dainty pink; and this time there was less trembling in the handwriting; and there was a greater frankness in the wording of the note.

"DEAR KEITH," Miss White wrote, "I would like to have the letters; as for the little trifles you mention, it does not much matter. You have not said that you forgive me; perhaps it is asking too much; but believe me you will find some day it was all for the best. It is better now than later on. I had my fears from the beginning; did not I tell you that I was never sure of myself for a day? And I am sure papa warned me. I cannot make you any requital for the great generosity and forbearance you show to me now; but I would like to be allowed to remain your friend.

"G. W."

"P.S.—I am deeply grieved to hear of your being ill; but hope it is only something quite temporary. You could not have decided better

than on taking a long sea-voyage. I hope you
will have fine weather."

All this was very pleasant. They had got
into the region of correspondence again : and
Miss White was then mistress of the situation.
His answer to her was less cheerful in tone.
It ran thus :—

"DEAR GERTRUDE,—To-morrow morning I
leave Dare. I have made up your letters, &c.,
in a packet ; but as I would like to see Norman
Ogilvie before going farther south, it is possible
we may run into the Thames for a day ; and
so I have taken the packet with me, and, if I
see Ogilvie, I will give it to him to put into
your hands. And as this may be the last time
that I shall ever write to you, I may tell you
now there is no one anywhere more earnestly
hopeful than I that you may live a long and
happy life, not troubled by any thinking of
what is past and irrevocable.

"Yours faithfully,

"KEITH MACLEOD."

So there was an end of correspondence. And
now came this beautiful morning, with a fine
north-westerly breeze blowing, and the *Umpire*,
with her mainsail and jib set, and her gay
ensign fluttering in the wind, rocking gently
down there at her moorings. It was an auspicious morning; of itself it was enough to cheer
up a heart-sick man. The white sea-birds were
calling; and Ulva was shining green; and the
Dutchman's Cap out there was of a pale purple-
blue; while away in the south there was a vague
silver mist of heat lying all over the Ross of
Mull and Iona. And the proud lady of Castle
Dare and Janet, and one or two others more
stealthily, were walking down to the pier to see
Keith Macleod set sail; but Donald was not
there — there was no need for Donald or his
pipes on board the yacht. Donald was up at
the house; and looking at the people going
down to the quay; and saying bitterly to
himself, "It is no more thought of the pipes
now that Sir Keith has, ever since the English
lady was at Dare; and he thinks I am better at
work in looking after the dogs."

Suddenly Macleod stopped, and took out a pencil, and wrote something on a card.

"I was sure I had forgotten something, Janet," said he. "That is the address of Johnny Wickes's mother. We were to send him up to see her some time before Christmas."

"Before Christmas!" Janet exclaimed; and she looked at him in amazement. "But you are coming back before Christmas, Keith!"

"Oh, well, Janet," said he carelessly, "you know that when one goes away on a voyage, it is never certain about your coming back at all, and it is better to leave everything right."

"But you are not going away from us with thoughts like these in your head, surely?" the cousin said. "Why, the man from Greenock says you could go to America in the *Umpire;* and if you could go to America, there will not be much risk in the calmer seas of the south. And you know, Keith, auntie and I don't want you to trouble about writing letters to us; for you will have enough trouble in looking after the yacht; but you will send us a telegram from the various places you put into."

"Oh, yes, I will do that," said he, somewhat absently. Even the bustle of departure and the brightness of the morning had failed to put colour and life into the haggard face and the hopeless eyes.

That was a sorrowful leave-taking at the shore ; and Macleod, standing on the deck of the yacht, could see, long after they had set sail, that his mother and cousin were still on the small quay watching the *Umpire* so long as she was in sight. Then they rounded the Ross of Mull ; and he saw no more of the women of Castle Dare.

And this beautiful white-sailed vessel that is going south through the summer seas : surely she is no deadly instrument of vengeance, but only a messenger of peace ? Look, now, how she has passed through the Sound of Iona : and the white sails are shining in the light ; and far away before her, instead of the islands with which she is familiar, are other islands—another Colonsay altogether, and Islay, and Jura, and Scarba, all a pale transparent blue. And what will the men on the lonely Dubh-Artach rock

THE *UMPIRE* SAILING SOUTH.

To face p. 230, col iii.

think of her as they see her pass by? Why, surely that she looks like a beautiful white dove! It is a summer day; the winds are soft; fly south, then, White Dove, and carry to her this message of tenderness, and entreaty, and peace! Surely the gentle ear will listen to you; before the winter comes, and the skies grow dark overhead, and there is no white dove at all, but an angry sea-eagle, with black wings outspread, and talons ready to strike. O what is the sound in the summer air? Is it the singing of the sea-maiden of Colonsay, bewailing still the loss of her lover in other years? We cannot stay to listen; the winds are fair; fly southward, and still southward, O you beautiful White Dove, and it is all a message of love and of peace that you will whisper to her ear!

CHAPTER XII.

DOVE OR SEA EAGLE ?

But there are no fine visions troubling the mind of Hamish as he stands here by the tiller in eager consultation with Colin Laing, who has a chart outspread before him on the deck. There is pride in the old man's face. He is proud of the performances of the yacht he has sailed for so many years; and proud of himself for having brought her—always subject to the advice of his cousin from Greenock—in safety through the salt sea to the smooth waters of the great river. And indeed this is a strange scene for the *Umpire* to find around her in the years of her old age. For instead of the giant cliffs of Gribun and Bourg there is only the thin green line

of the Essex coast; and instead of the rushing Atlantic there is the broad smooth surface
of this coffee-coloured stream, splashed with
blue where the ripples catch the reflected
light of the sky. There is no longer the
solitude of Ulva and Colonsay, or the moan-
ing of the waves round the lonely shores
of Fladda, and Staffa, and the Dutchman;
but the eager, busy life of the great river—a
black steamer puffing and roaring, russet-
sailed barges going smoothly with the tide, a
tug bearing a large green-hulled Italian ship
through the lapping waters, and everywhere
a swarming fry of small boats of every description. It is a beautiful summer morning,
though there is a pale haze lying along the
Essex woods. The old *Umpire*, with the salt
foam of the sea encrusted on her bows, is
making her first appearance in the Thames.

"And where are we going, Hamish," says
Colin Laing, in the Gaelic, "when we leave
this place?"

"When you are told, then you will know,"
says Hamish.

" You had enough talk of it last night in the cabin. I thought you were never coming out of the cabin," says the cousin from Greenock.

" And if I have a master, I obey my master without speaking," Hamish answers.

" Well, it is a strange master you have got. Oh, you do not know about these things, Hamish. Do you know what a gentleman who has a yacht would do when he got into Gravesend as we got in last night? Why he would go ashore, and have his dinner in a hotel, and drink four or five different kinds of wine, and go to the theatre. But your master, Hamish, what does he do? He stays on board; and sends ashore for time-tables, and such things; and what is more than that, he is on deck all night, walking up and down. Oh, yes, I heard him walking up and down all night, with the yacht lying at anchor ! "

" Sir Keith is not well. When a man is not well he does not act in an ordinary way. But you talk of my master," Hamish answered proudly. " Well, I will tell you about my master, Colin—that he is a better master than any ten thousand masters that ever were born in Greenock, or in London either. I will not allow any man to say anything against my master."

" I was not saying anything against your master. He is a wiser man than you, Hamish. For he was saying to me last night, ' Now, when I am sending Hamish to such and such places in London, you must go with him, and show him the trains, and cabs, and other things like that.' Oh yes, Hamish, you know how to sail a yacht; but you do not know anything about towns."

" And who would want to know anything about towns ? Are they not full of people who live by telling lies and cheating each other ? "

" And do you say that is how I have been able to buy my house at Gourock," said Colin Laing, angrily, " with a garden, and a boat-house too ? "

" I do not know about that," said Hamish ; and then he called out some order to one of the

men. Macleod was at this moment down in the
saloon, seated at the table, with a letter enclosed
and addressed lying before him.   But surely this
was not the same man who had been in these
still waters of the Thames in the bygone days—
with gay companions around him, and the
band playing "A Highland Lad my Love
was born," and a beautiful-eyed girl, whom he
called Rose-leaf, talking to him in the quiet of
the summer noon.   This man had a look in his
eyes like that of an animal that has been hunted
to death and is fain to lie down and give itself
up to its pursuers in the despair of utter fatigue.
He was looking at this letter. The composition
of it had cost him only a whole night's agony.
And when he sate down and wrote it in the blue-
grey dawn, what had he not cast away ?

" Oh, no," he was saying now to his own con-
science, " she will not call it deceiving ! She
will laugh when it is all over—she will call it a
stratagem—she will say that a drowning man
will catch at anything.   And this is the last
effort—but it is only a stratagem : she herself
will absolve me—when she laughs and says,

'Oh, how could you have treated the poor theatres so ? ' "

A loud rattling overhead startled him.

" We must be at Erith," he said to himself; and then, after a pause of a second, he took the letter in his hand. He passed up the companion-way; perhaps it was the sudden glare of the light around that falsely gave to his eyes the appearance of a man who had been drinking hard. But his voice was clear and precise as he said to Hamish—

" Now, Hamish, you understand everything I have told you ? "

" Oh, yes, Sir Keith."

" And you will put away that nonsense from your head; and when you see the English lady that you remember, you will be very respectful to her, for she is a very great friend of mine; and if she is not at the theatre, you will go on to the other address, and Colin Laing will go with you in the cab. And if she comes back in the cab, you and Colin will go outside beside the driver, do you understand ? And when you go ashore, you will take John Cameron with you, and you will ask the pier-master about the moorings."

"Oh, yes, Sir Keith; have you not told me before?" Hamish said, almost reproachfully.

"You are sure you got everything on board last night?"

"There is nothing more that I can think of, Sir Keith."

"Here is the letter, Hamish."

And so he pledged himself to the last desperate venture.

Not long after that Hamish, and Laing, and John Cameron went in the dingay to the end of Erith pier; and left the boat there; and went along to the head of the pier, and had a talk with the pier-master. Then John Cameron returned to the yacht; and the other two went on their way to the railway-station.

"And I will tell you this, Hamish," said the little black Celt, who swaggered a good deal in his walk, "that when you go in the train you will be greatly frightened. For you do not know how strong the engines are; and how they will carry you through the air."

"That is a foolish thing to say," answered Hamish, also speaking in the Gaelic; "for I have seen many pictures of trains; and do you say that the engines are bigger than the engines of the *Pioneer* or the *Dunara Castle* or the *Clansman* that goes to Stornoway? Do not talk such nonsense to me. An engine that runs along the road, that is a small matter; but an engine that can take you up the Sound of Sleat, and across the Minch, and all the way to Stornoway, that is an engine to be talked about!"

But nevertheless it was with some inward trepidation that Hamish approached Erith station; and it was with an awestruck silence that he saw his cousin take tickets at the office; nor did he speak a word when the train came up and they entered and sate down in the carriage. Then the train moved off, and Hamish breathed more freely: what was this to be afraid of?

"Did I not tell you you would be frightened?" Colin Laing said.

"I am not frightened at all," Hamish answered, indignantly.

But as the train began to move more quickly, Hamish's hands, that held firmly by the wooden seat on which he was sitting, tightened, and still further tightened, their grasp; and his teeth got clenched; while there was an anxious look in his eyes. At length, as the train swung into a good pace, his fear got the better of him, and he called out—

"Colin—Colin—she's run away!"

And then Colin Laing laughed aloud; and began to assume great airs; and told Hamish that he was no better than a lad kept for herding the sheep who had never been away from his own home. This familiar air reassured Hamish; and then the train stopping at Abbey Wood proved to him that the engine was still under control.

"Oh, yes, Hamish," continued his travelled cousin, "you will open your eyes when you see London; and you will tell all the people when you go back that you have never seen so great a place; but what is London to the cities and the towns and the palaces that I have seen? Did you ever hear of Valparaiso, Hamish? Oh, yes, you will live a long time before you

will get to Valparaiso ! And Rio : why, I have
known mere boys that have been to Rio. And
you can sail a yacht very well, Hamish ; and
I do not grumble that you would be the master
of the yacht—though I know the banks and
the channels a little better than you ; and it
was quite right of you to be the master of the
yacht; but you have not seen what I have
seen. And I have been where there are
mountains and mountains of gold——"

"Do you take me for a fool, Colin ?" said
Hamish, with a contemptuous smile.

"Not quite that," said the other; "but am
I not to believe my own eyes ?"

"And if there were the great mountains of
gold," said Hamish, "why did you not fill your
pockets with the gold ; and would not that be
better than selling whisky in Greenock ?"

"Yes ; and that shows what an ignorant man
you are, Hamish," said the other with disdain.
"For do you not know that the gold is mixed
with quartz, and you have got to take the
quartz out ? But I dare say now you do not
know what quartz is : for it is a very ignorant

man you are, although you can sail a yacht.
But I do not grumble at all. You are master
of your own yacht; just as I am the master
of my own shop. But if you were coming into
my shop, Hamish, I would say to you, 'Hamish,
you are the master here; and I am not the
master; and you can take a glass of anything
you like.' That is what people who have travelled
all over the world, and seen princes and great
cities and palaces, call *politeness*. But how
could you know anything about *politeness?*
You have lived only on the west coast of Mull;
and they do not even know how to speak good
Gaelic there."

"That is a lie, Colin," said Hamish, with
decision. "We have better Gaelic there than
any other Gaelic that is spoken."

"Were you ever in Lochaber, Hamish?"

"No, I was never in Lochaber."

"Then do not pretend to give an opinion
about the Gaelic—especially to a man who
has travelled all over the world, though
perhaps he cannot sail a yacht as well as
you, Hamish."

The two cousins soon grew friends again, however. And now, as they were approaching London, a strange thing became visible. The blue sky became obscured. The whole world seemed to be enveloped in a clear brown haze of smoke.

"Ay, ay," said Hamish, "that is a strange thing."

"What is a strange thing, Hamish?"

"I was reading about it in a book many a time—the great fire that was burning in London for years and years and years: and have they not quite got it out, Colin?"

"I do not know what you are talking about, Hamish," said the other, who had not much book-learning, "but I will tell you this, that you may prepare yourself now to open your eyes. Oh, yes, London will make you open your eyes wide; though it is nothing to one who has been to Rio, and Shanghai, and Rotterdam, and other places like that."

Now these references to foreign parts only stung Hamish's pride; and when they did arrive at London Bridge he was determined

to show no surprise whatever. He stepped
into the four-wheeled cab that Colin Laing
chartered, just as if four-wheeled cabs were
as common as sea-gulls on the shores of
Loch-na-Keal. And though his eyes were
bewildered and his ears dinned with the
wonderful sights and sounds of this great
roaring city—that seemed to have the popu-
lation of all the world pouring through its
streets—he would say nothing at all. At last
the cab stopped; the two men were opposite
the Piccadilly Theatre.

Then Hamish got out and left his cousin
with the cab. He ascended the wide steps;
he entered the great vestibule; and he had a
letter in his hand. The old man had not
trembled so much since he was a schoolboy.

"What do you want, my man?" some one
said, coming out of the box-office by chance.

Hamish showed the letter.

"I wass to hef an answer, sir, if you please,
sir, and I will be obliged," said Hamish, who
had been enjoined to be very courteous.

"Take it round to the stage-entrance," said the man, carelessly.

"Yes, sir, if you please, sir," said Hamish; but he did not understand; and he stood still.

The man looked at him; called for some one; a young lad came; and to him was given the letter.

"You may wait here, then," said he to Hamish, "but I think rehearsal is over, and Miss White has most likely gone home."

The man went into the box-office again; Hamish was left alone there, in the great empty vestibule. The Piccadilly Theatre had seldom seen within its walls a more picturesque figure than this old Highlandman, who stood there with his sailor's cap in his hand, and with a keen excitement in the proud and fine face. There was a watchfulness in the grey eyes like the watchfulness of an eagle. If he twisted his cap rather nervously, and if his heart beat quick, it was not from fear.

Now when the letter was brought to Miss White, she was standing in one of the wings, laughing and chatting with the stage manager.

The laugh went from her face. She grew quite pale.

"Oh, Mr. Cartwright," said she, "do you think I could go down to Erith and be back before six in the evening?"

"Oh, yes; why not?" said he, carelessly.

But she scarcely heard him. She was still staring at that sheet of paper, with its piteous cry of the sick man. Only to see her once more —to shake hands in token of forgiveness—to say good-bye for the last time: what woman with the heart of a woman could resist the despairing prayer?

"Where is the man who brought this letter?" said she.

"In front, miss," said the young lad, "by the box-office."

Very quickly she made her way along the gloomy and empty corridors, and there in the twilit hall she found the grey-haired old sailor with his cap held humbly in his hands.

"Oh, Hamish," said she, "is Sir Keith so very ill?"

"Is it ill, mem?" said Hamish; and quick tears sprang to the old man's eyes. "He iss more ill than you can think of, mem; it iss another man that he iss now. Ay, ay, who would know him to be Sir Keith Macleod?"

"He wants me to go and see him— and I suppose I have no time to go home first——"

"Here is the list of the trains, mem," said Hamish, eagerly, producing a certain card. "And it iss me and Colin Laing, that's my cousin, mem; and we hef a cab outside; and will you go to the station! Oh, you will not know Sir Keith, mem; there iss no one at all would know my master now."

"Come along, then, Hamish," said she, quickly. "Oh, but he cannot be so ill as that. And the long sea-voyage will pull him round, don't you think?"

"Ay, ay, mem," said Hamish; but he was paying little heed. He called up the cab; and Miss White stepped inside; and he and Colin Laing got on the box.

"Tell him to go quickly," she said to Hamish,

"for I must have some scrap of luncheon if we
have a minute at the station."

And Miss White, as the cab rolled away, felt
pleased with herself. It was a brave act.

"It is the least I can do for the sake of my
bonnie Glenogie," she was saying to herself,
quite cheerfully. "And if Mr. Lemuel were
to hear of it? Well, he must know that I
mean to be mistress of my own conduct. And
so the poor Glenogie is really ill. I can do no
harm in parting good friends with him. Some
men would have made a fuss."

At the station they had ten minutes to wait;
and Miss White was able to get the slight re-
freshment she desired. And although Hamish
would fain have kept out of her way—for it
was not becoming in a rude sailor to be seen
speaking to so fine a lady—she would not
allow that.

"And where are you going, Hamish, when
you leave the Thames?" she asked, smoothing
the fingers of the glove she had just put on
again.

"I do not know that, mem," said he.

"I hope Sir Keith won't go to Torquay or any of those languid places. You will go to the Mediterranean, I suppose?"

"Maybe that will be the place, mem," said Hamish.

"Or the Isle of Wight, perhaps," said she, carelessly.

"Ay, ay, mem—the Isle of Wight—that will be a ferry good place now. There wass a man I wass seeing once in Tobbermorry, and he wass telling me about the castle that the Queen herself will hef on that island. And Mr. Ross, the Queen's piper, he will be living there too."

But, of course, they had to part company when the train came up; and Hamish and Colin Laing got into a third-class carriage together. The cousin from Greenock had been hanging rather in the background; but he had kept his ears open.

"Now, Hamish," said he, in the tongue in which they could both speak freely enough, "I will tell you something; and do not think I am an ignorant man; for I know what is going on.

Oh, yes. And it is a great danger you are running into."

"What do you mean, Colin?" said Hamish; but he would look out of the window.

"When a gentleman goes away in a yacht, does he take an old woman like Christina with him? Oh no; I think not. It is not a customary thing. And the ladies' cabin; the ladies' cabin is kept very smart, Hamish. And I think I know who is to have the ladies' cabin."

"Then you are very clever, Colin," said Hamish, contemptuously. "But it is too clever you are. You think it strange that the young English lady should take that cabin. I will tell you this—that it is not the first time nor the second time that the young English lady has gone for a voyage in the *Umpire*, and in that very cabin too. And I will tell you this, Colin; that it is this very year she had that cabin; and was in Loch Tua, and Loch-na-Keal, and Loch Scridain, and Calgary Bay. And as for Christina —oh, it is much you know about fine ladies in Greenock! I tell you that an English lady cannot go anywhere without some one to attend to her."

"Hamish, do not try to make a fool of me," said Laing, angrily. "Do you think a lady would go travelling without any luggage? And she does not know where the *Umpire* is going!"

"Do you know?"

"No."

"Very well, then. It is Sir Keith Macleod who is the master when he is on board the *Umpire*, and where he wants to go, the others have to go."

"Oh, do you think that? And do you speak like that to a man who can pay eighty-five pounds a year of rent?"

"No, I do not forget that it is a kindness to me that you are doing, Colin; and to Sir Keith Macleod, too; and he will not forget it. But as for this young lady, or that young lady, what has that to do with it? You know what the bell of Scoon said, '*That which concerns you not, meddle not with.*'"

"I shall be glad when I am back in Greenock," said Colin Laing, moodily.

But was not this a fine, fair scene that Miss

Gertrude White saw around her when they came in sight of the river and Erith pier ?—the flashes of blue on the water, the white-sailed yachts, the russet-sailed barges, and the sunlight shining all along the thin line of the Essex shore. The moment she set foot on the pier she recognised the *Umpire* lying out there, the great white mainsail and jib idly flapping in the summer breeze : but there was no one on deck. And she was not afraid at all; for had he not written in so kindly a fashion to her ; and was she not doing much for his sake, too ?

"Will the shock be great ?" she was thinking to herself. "I hope my bonnie Glenogie is not so ill as that ; for he always looked like a man. And it is so much better that we should part good friends."

She turned to Hamish.

"There is no one on the deck of the yacht, Hamish," said she.

"No, mem," said he, "the men will be at the end of the pier, mem, in the boat, if you please, mem."

"Then you took it for granted I should come back with you?" said she, with a pleasant smile.

"I wass thinking you would come to see Sir Keith, mem," said Hamish, gravely. His manner was very respectful to the fine English lady; but there was not much of friendliness in his look.

She followed Hamish down the rude wooden steps at the end of the pier; and there they found the dingay awaiting them, with two men in her. Hamish was very careful of Miss White's dress as she got into the stern of the boat; then he and Colin Laing got into the bow; and the men half paddled and half floated her along to the *Umpire*—the tide having begun to ebb.

And it was with much ceremony, too, that Hamish assisted Miss White to get on board by the little gangway; and for a second or two she stood on deck and looked around her while the men were securing the dingay. The idlers lounging on Erith pier must have considered that this was an additional feature of interest in the

summer picture—the figure of this pretty young
lady standing there on the white decks and looking around her with a pleased curiosity. It was
some little time since she had been on board the
Umpire.

Then Hamish turned to her, and said, in the
same respectful way—

" Will you go below, mem, now? It iss in
the saloon that you will find Sir Keith, and if
Christina iss in the way, you will tell her to go
away, mem."

The small gloved hand was laid on the top of
the companion, and Miss White carefully went
down the wooden steps. And it was with a
gentleness equal to her own that Hamish shut
the little doors after her.

But no sooner had she quite disappeared than
the old man's manner swiftly changed. He
caught hold of the companion-hatch; jammed
it across with a noise that was heard throughout
the whole vessel; and then he sprang to the
helm, with the keen grey eyes afire with a wild
excitement.

" Damn her, we have her now!" he said,

between his teeth; and he called aloud: "Haul in the weather jib-sheet there! Let go the moorings, John Cameron! God damn her, we have her now!—and it is not yet that she has put a shame on Macleod of Dare!"

CHAPTER XIII.

THE PRISONER.

THE sudden noise overhead and the hurried tramp of the men on deck were startling enough; but surely there was nothing to alarm her in the calm and serious face of this man who stood before her. He did not advance towards her. He regarded her with a sad tenderness—as if he were looking at one far away. When the beloved dead come back to us in the wonder-halls of sleep, there is no wild joy of meeting. There is something strange. And when they disappear again, there is no surprise : only the dull aching returns to the heart.

"Gertrude," said he, "you are as safe here as ever you were in your mother's arms. No one will harm you."

"What is it? What do you mean?" said she, quickly.

She was somewhat bewildered. She had not expected to meet him thus suddenly face to face. And then she became aware that the companion-way by which she had descended into the saloon had grown dark: that was the meaning of the harsh noise.

"I want to go ashore, Keith," said she, hurriedly. "Put me on shore. I will speak to you there."

"You cannot go ashore," said he, calmly.

"I don't know what you mean," said she; and her heart began to beat fast. "I tell you I want to go ashore, Keith. I will speak to you there."

"You cannot go ashore, Gertrude," he repeated. "We have already left Erith. . . . Gerty, Gerty," he continued, for she was struck dumb with a sudden terror, "don't you understand now? I have stolen you away from yourself. There was but the one thing left: the one way of saving you. And you will forgive me, Gerty, when you understand it all——"

She was gradually recovering from her terror. She did understand it now. And he was not ill at all?

"Oh, you coward!—you coward!—you coward!" she exclaimed, with a blaze of fury in her eyes. "And I was to confer a kindness on you—a last kindness! But you dare not do this thing—I tell you, you dare not do it! I demand to be put on shore at once. Do you hear me?"

She turned wildly round, as if to seek for some way of escape. The door in the ladies' cabin stood open; the daylight was streaming down into that bright little place; there were some flowers on the dressing-table. But the way by which she had descended was barred over and dark.

She faced him again; and her eyes were full of fierce indignation and anger; she drew herself up to her full height; she overwhelmed him with taunts, and reproaches, and scorn. That was a splendid piece of acting, seeing that it had never been rehearsed. He stood unmoved before all this theatrical rage.

"Oh, yes, you were proud of your name," she

was saying, with bitter emphasis, "and I thought you belonged to a race of gentlemen, to whom lying was unknown. And you were no longer murderous and revengeful; but you can take your revenge on a woman, for all that! And you ask me to come and see you, because you are ill! And you have laid a trap—like a coward!"

"And if I am what you say, Gerty," said he, quite gently, "it is the love of you that has made me that. Oh, you do not know!"

She saw nothing of the lines that pain had written on this man's face; she recognised nothing of the very majesty of grief in the hopeless eyes. He was only her jailer, her enemy.

"Of course—of course," said she. "It is the woman—it is always the woman who is in fault! That is a manly thing—to put the blame on the woman! And it is a manly thing to take your revenge on a woman! I thought when a man had a rival that it was his rival whom he sought out. But you—you kept out of the way——"

He strode forward, and caught her by the

wrist. There was a look in his face that for
a second terrified her into silence.

"Gerty," said he, "I warn you. Do not mention that man to me—now or at any time; or
it will be bad for him and for you."

She twisted her hand from his grasp.

"How dare you come near me!" she cried.

"I beg your pardon," said he, with an instant
return to his former grave gentleness of manner.
"I wish to let you know how you are situated,
if you will let me, Gerty. I don't wish to justify
what I have done; for you would not hear me—
just yet. But this I must tell you, that I don't
wish to force myself on your society. You will
do as you please. There is your cabin; you have
occupied it before. If you would like to have
this saloon, you can have that, too : I mean I
shall not come into it, unless it pleases you.
And there is a bell in your cabin; and if you
ring it, Christina will answer."

She heard him out patiently; her reply was
a scornful—perhaps nervous—laugh.

"Why, this is mere folly," she exclaimed.
"It is simple madness. I begin to believe that

you are really ill, after all ; and it is your mind that is affected. Surely you don't know what you are doing ?"

" You are angry, Gerty," said he.

But the first blaze of her wrath and indignation had passed away ; and now fear was coming uppermost.

" Surely, Keith, you cannot be dreaming of such a mad thing ! Oh, it is impossible. It is a joke ; it was to frighten me : it was to punish me, perhaps ? Well, I have deserved it ; but now—now you have succeeded ; and you will let me go ashore, further down the river."

Her tone was altered. She had been watching his face.

"Oh no, Gerty, oh no," he said. "Do you not understand yet ? You were everything in the world to me—you were life itself—without you I had nothing, and the world might just as well come to an end for me. And when I thought you were going away from me, what could I do ? I could not reach you by letters, and letters ; and how could I know what the people around you were saying to you ? Ah, you do not know what I have suffered, Gerty; and always I was saying to myself that if I could get you away from these people, you would remember the time that you gave me the red rose, and all those beautiful days would come back again, and I would take your hand again, and I would forget altogether about the terrible nights when I seemed to see you beside me and heard you laugh just as in the old times. And I knew there was only the one way left. How could I but try that? I knew you would be angry; but I hoped your anger would go away. And now you are angry, Gerty, and my speaking to you is not of much use—as yet; but I can wait until I see you yourself again, as you used to be, in the garden —don't you remember, Gerty?"

Her face was proud, cold, implacable.

"Do I understand you aright—that you have shut me up in this yacht and mean to take me away?"

"Gerty, I have saved you from yourself!"

"Will you be so kind as to tell me where we are going?"

"Why not away back to the Highlands, Gerty?" said he, eagerly. "And then some day when your heart relents, and you forgive me, you will put your hand in mine, and we will walk up the road to Castle Dare. Do you not think they will be glad to see us that day, Gerty?"

She maintained her proud attitude; but she was trembling from head to foot.

"Do you mean to say that until I consent to be your wife I am not to be allowed to leave this yacht?"

"You will consent, Gerty!"

"Not if I were to be shut up here for a thousand years!" she exclaimed, with another burst of passion. "Oh, you will pay for this dearly! I thought it was madness—mere folly; but if it is true, you will rue this day! Do you think we are savages here?—do you think we have no law?"

"I do not care for any law," said he simply. "I can only think of the one thing in the world: if I have not your love, Gerty, what else can I care about?"

"My love!" she exclaimed. "And this is the way to earn it, truly! My love! If you were to keep me shut up for a thousand years, you would never have it! You can have my hatred, if you like; and plenty of it, too."

"You are angry, Gerty," was all he said.

"Oh, you do not know with whom you have to deal!" she continued, with the same bitter emphasis. "You terrified me with stories of butchery—the butchery of innocent women and children; and no doubt you thought the stories were fine; and now you too would show you are one of the race by taking revenge on a woman. But if she is only a woman, you have not conquered her yet! Oh, you will find out before long that we have law in this country, and that it is not to be outraged with impunity. You think you can do as you like; because you are a Highland master, and you have a lot of slaves round you!"

"I am going on deck now, Gerty," said he, in the same sad and gentle way. "You are tiring yourself. Shall I send Christina to you?"

For an instant she looked bewildered, as if she
had not till now comprehended what was going
on ; and then she said, quite wildly—

" Oh, no, no, no, Keith ; you don't mean what
you say ! You cannot mean it ! You are only
frightening me ! You will put me ashore—and
not a word shall pass my lips. We cannot be
far down the river, Keith. There are many
places where you could put me ashore ; and
I could get back to London by rail. They
won't know I have ever seen you. Keith, you
will put me ashore now ! "

" And if I were to put you ashore now, you
would go away, Gerty, and I should never see
you again—never, and never. And what would
that be for you and for me, Gerty ? But now
you are here, no one can poison your mind ;
you will be angry for a time ; but the brighter
days are coming—oh, yes, I know that : if I was
not sure of that, what would become of me ? It
is a good thing to have hope ; to look forward
to the glad days ; that stills the pain at the
heart. And now we two are together at last,
Gerty !—and if you are angry, the anger will

pass away; and we will go forward together to the glad days."

She was listening in a sort of vague and stunned amazement. Both her anger and her fear were slowly yielding to the bewilderment of the fact that she was really setting out on a voyage, the end of which neither she nor any one living could know.

"Ah, Gerty," said he, regarding her with a strange wistfulness in the sad eyes, "you do not know what it is to me to see you again. I have seen you many a time—in dreams; but you were always far away; and I could not take your hand. And I said to myself that you were not cruel; that you did not wish any one to suffer pain; and I knew if I could only see you again, and take you away from these people, then your heart would be gentle, and you would think of the time when you gave me the red rose, and we went out in the garden, and all the air round us was so full of gladness that we did not speak at all. Oh, yes; and I said to myself that your true friends were in the north; and what would the men at Dubh-artach not

do for you, and Captain Macallum, too, when
they knew you were coming to live at Dare;
and I was thinking that would be a grand day
when you came to live among us; and there
would be dancing, and a good glass of whisky
for every one, and some playing on the pipes
that day! And sometimes I did not know
whether there would be more of laughing or
of crying when Janet came to meet you. But
I will not trouble you any more now, Gerty;
for you are tired I think; and I will send
Christina to you. And you will soon think
that I was not cruel to you when I took you
away and saved you from yourself."

She did not answer; she seemed in a sort
of trance. But she was aroused by the entrance
of Christina, who came in directly after Macleod
left. Miss White stared at this white-haired
woman, as if uncertain how to address her; when
she spoke it was in a friendly and persuasive way.

"You have not forgotten me, then, Christina?"

"No, mem," said the grave Highland woman:
she had beautiful, clear, blue-grey eyes, but there
was no pity in them.

"I suppose you have no part in this mad freak?"

The old woman seemed puzzled. She said, with a sort of serious politeness—

"I do not know, mem. I have not the good English as Hamish."

"But surely you know this," said Miss Gertrude White, with more animation, "that I am here against my will? You understand that, surely? That I am being carried away against my will from my own home and my friends? You know it very well; but perhaps your master has not told you of the risk you run? Do you know what that is? Do you think there are no laws in this country?"

"Sir Keith he is the master of the boat," said Christina. "Iss there anything now that I can do for you, mem?"

"Yes," said Miss White, boldly. "There is. You can help me to get ashore. And you will save your master from being looked on as a madman. And you will save yourselves from being hanged."

"I wass to ask you," said the old Highland

woman, "when you would be for having the dinner. And Hamish, he wass saying that you will hef the dinner what time you are thinking of ; and will you hef the dinner all by yourself?"

"I tell you this, woman," said Miss White, with quick anger, "that I will neither eat nor drink so long as I am on board this yacht! What is the use of such nonsense! I wish to be put on shore. I am getting tired of this folly. I tell you I want to go ashore ; and I am going ashore ; and it will be the worse for any one who tries to stop me."

"I think you not can go ashore, mem," Christina said, somewhat deliberately picking out her English phrases. "For the gig iss up at the davits now ; and the dingay—you wass not thinking of going ashore by yourself in the dingay? And last night, mem, at a town, we had many things brought on board ; and if you wass tell me what you will hef for the dinner, there is no one more willing than me. And I hope you will hef very good comfort on board the yacht."

"I can't get it into your head that you are

s 2

talking nonsense," said Miss White, angrily. "I
tell you I will not go anywhere in the yacht!
And what is the use of talking to me about
dinner? I tell you I will neither eat nor drink
while I am on board this yacht."

"I think that will be a ferry foolish thing,
mem," Christina said, humbly enough; but all
the same the scornful fashion in which this
young lady had addressed her had stirred a
little of the Highland woman's blood; and she
added—still with great apparent humility—
"But if you will not eat, they say that iss
a ferry good thing for the pride; and there iss
not much pride left if one hass nothing to
eat, mem."

"I presume that is to be my prison?" said
Miss White, haughtily, turning to the smart
little state-room beyond the companion.

"That iss your cabin, mem, if you please,
mem," said Christina, who had been instructed
in English politeness by her husband.

"Well, now, can you understand this? Go
to Sir Keith Macleod, and tell him that I have
shut myself up in that cabin; and that I will

speak not a word to any one; and I will neither eat nor drink, until I am taken on shore. And so, if he wishes to have a murder on his hands, very well! Do you understand that?"

"I will say that to Sir Keith," Christina answered submissively.

Miss White walked into the cabin; and locked herself in. It was an apartment with which she was familiar; but where had they got the white heather? And there were books; but she paid little heed. They would discover they had not broken her spirit yet.

On both sides the skylight overhead was open an inch; and it was nearer to the tiller than the skylight of the saloon. In the absolute stillness of this summer day she heard two men talking. Generally, they spoke in the Gaelic, which was of course unintelligible to her; but sometimes they wandered into English — especially if the name of some English town cropped up—and thus she got hints as to the whereabouts of the *Umpire*.

"Oh, yes, it is a fine big town that town of Gravesend, to be sure, Hamish," said the one voice, "and I have no doubt, now, that it will be sending a gentleman to the Houses of Parliament in London, just as Greenock will do. But there is no one you will send from Mull. They do not know much about Mull in the Houses of Parliament!"

"And they know plenty about ferry much worse places," said Hamish proudly. "And wass you saying there will be anything so beautiful about Greenock as you will find at Tobbermorry?"

"Tobermory!" said the other. "There are some trees at Tobermory—oh, yes; and the Mish-nish and the shops——"

"Yess, and the water-fahl—do not forget the water-fahl, Colin; and there iss better whisky in Tobbermorry ass you will get in all Greenock, where they will be for mixing it with prandy and other drinks like that; and at Tobbermorry you will hef a Professor come ahl the way from Edinburgh and from Oban to gif a lecture on the Gaelic; but do you think he would gif a lecture in a town like Greenock? Oh, no; he would not do that!"

" Very well, Hamish; but it is glad I am that we are going back the way we came."

" And me, too, Colin."

" And I will not be sorry when I am in Greenock once more."

" But you will come with us first of all to Castle Dare, Colin," was the reply. " And I know that Lady Macleod herself will be for shaking hands with you, and thanking you that you wass tek the care of the yacht."

" I think I will stop at Greenock, Hamish. You know you can take her well on from Greenock. And will you go round the Mull, Hamish, or through the Crinan, do you think now ? "

" Oh, I am not afrait to tek her round the Moil; but there is the English lady on board; and it will be smoother for her to go through the Crinan. And it iss ferry glad I will be, Colin, to see Ardalanish Point again; for I would rather be going through the Doruis Mohr twenty times ass getting petween the panks of this tamned river."

Here they relapsed into their native tongue,

and she listened no longer; but at all events she had learned that they were going away to the north. And as her nerves had been somewhat shaken, she began to ask herself what further thing this madman might not do. The old stories he had told her came back with a marvellous distinctness. Would he plunge her into a dungeon and mock her with an empty cup when she was dying of thirst? Would he chain her to a rock at low water and watch the tide slowly rise? He professed great gentleness and love for her; but if the savage nature had broken out at last? Her fear grew apace. He had shown himself regardless of everything on earth: where would he stop, if she continued to repel him? And then the thought of her situation—alone; shut up in this small room; about to venture forth on the open sea with this ignorant crew—so overcame her that she hastily snatched at the bell on the dressing-table, and rang it violently. Almost instantly there was a tapping at the door.

"I ask your pardon, mem," she heard Christina say.

She sprang to the door, and opened it, and caught the arm of the old woman.

"Christina, Christina," she said, almost wildly, "you won't let them take me away! My father will give you hundreds and hundreds of pounds if only you get me ashore. Just think of him— he is an old man—if you had a daughter——"

Miss White was acting very well indeed; though she was more concerned about herself than her father.

"I wass to say to you," Christina explained with some difficulty, "that if you wass saying that, Sir Keith had a message sent away to your father, and you wass not to think any more about that. And now, mem, I cannot tek you ashore; it iss no business I hef with that; and I could not go ashore myself whateffer; but I would get you some dinner, mem."

"Then I suppose you don't understand the English language!" Miss White exclaimed, angrily. "I tell you I will neither eat nor drink so long as I am on board this yacht. Go and tell Sir Keith Macleod what I have said!"

So Miss White was left alone again ; and the slow time passed ; and she heard the murmured conversation of the men ; and also a measured pacing to and fro which she took to be the step of Macleod. Quick rushes of feeling went through her—indignation ; a stubborn obstinacy ; a wonder over the audacity of this thing ; malevolent hatred even ; but all these were being gradually subdued by the dominant claim of hunger. Miss White had acted the part of many heroines ; but she was not herself a heroine—if there is anything heroic in starvation. It was growing to dusk when she again summoned the old Highlandwoman.

"Get me something to eat," said she ; "I cannot die like a rat in a hole."

"Yes, mem," said Christina, in the most matter-of-fact way—for she had never been in a theatre in her life, and she had not imagined that Miss White's threat meant anything at all. "The dinner is just ready now, mem ; and if you will hef it in the saloon, there will be no one there ; that wass Sir Keith's message to you."

"I will not have it in the saloon; I will have it here."

"Ferry well, mem," Christina said, submissively. "But you will go into the saloon, mem, when I will mek the bed for you, and the lamp will hef to be lit, but Hamish he will light the lamp for you. And is there any other things you wass thinking of that you would like, mem?"

"No; I want something to eat."

"And Hamish, mem, he wass saying I will ask you whether you will hef the claret-wine, or—or—the other wine, mem, that meks a noise——"

"Bring me some water. But the whole of you will pay dearly for this!"

"I ask your pardon, mem?" said Christina, with great respect.

"Oh, go away, and get me something to eat."

And in fact Miss White made a very good dinner, though the things had to be placed before her on her dressing-table. And her rage and indignation did not prevent her having, after all, a glass or two of the claret-wine. And then she permitted Hamish to come in and light the swinging-lamp; and thereafter Christina made up one of the two narrow beds. Miss White was left alone.

Many a hundred times had she been placed in great peril—on the stage; and she knew that on such occasions it had been her duty to clasp her hand on her forehead and set to work to find out how to extricate herself. Well, on this occasion, she did not make use of any dramatic gesture; but she turned out the lamp; and threw herself on the top of the narrow little bed; and was determined that, before they got her conveyed to their savage home in the north, she would make one more effort for her freedom. Then she heard the man at the helm begin to hum to himself "*Fhir a bhata, na horo eile.*" The night darkened. And soon all the wild emotions of the day were forgotten; for she was asleep.

* * * *

Asleep—in the very waters through which she had sailed with her lover on the white summer day. But *Rose-leaf—Rose-leaf—what faint wind will carry you* NOW *to the south* ?

CHAPTER XLV.

AND now the brave old *Umpire* is nearing her northern home once more; and surely this is a right royal evening for the reception of her. What although the sun has just gone down, and the sea around them become a plain of heaving and wrestling blue-black waves? Far away, in that purple-black sea, lie long promontories that are of a still pale rose-colour; and the western sky is a blaze of golden-green; and they know that the wild, beautiful radiance is still touching the wan walls of Castle Dare. And there is Ardalanish Point; and that the ruddy Ross of Mull; and there will be a good tide in the Sound of Iona. Why, then, do they linger, and keep the old *Umpire* with her sails flapping idly in the wind?

As you pass through Jura's Sound
Bend your course by Scarba's shore ;
Shun, O shun, the gulf profound
Where Corrievreckan's surges roar !

They are in no danger of Corrievreckan now ; they are in familiar waters ; only that is another Colonsay that lies away there in the south. Keith Macleod, seated up at the bow, is calmly regarding it. He is quite alone. There is no sound around him but the lapping of the waves.

And ever as the year returns,
The charm-bound sailors know the day ;
For sadly still the Mermaid mourns
The lovely chief of Colonsay.

And is he listening now for the wild sound of her singing ? Or is he thinking of the brave Macphail who went back after seven long months of absence, and found the maid of Colonsay still true to him ? The ruby ring she had given him had never paled. There was one woman who could remain true to her absent lover.

Hamish came forward.

"Will we go on now, sir?" said he, in the Gaelic.

"No."

Hamish looked round. The shining clear evening looked very calm, notwithstanding the tossing of the blue-black waves. And it seemed wasteful to the old sailor to keep the yacht lying-to or aimlessly sailing this way and that while this favourable wind remained to them.

"I am not sure that the breeze will last, Sir Keith."

"Are you sure of anything, Hamish?" Macleod said, quite absently. "Well, there is one thing we can all make sure of. But I have told you, Hamish, I am not going up the Sound of Iona in daylight: why, there is not a man in all the islands who would not know of our coming by to-morrow morning. We will go up the Sound as soon as it is dark. It is a new moon to-night. And I think we can go without lights, Hamish."

"The *Dunara* is coming south to-night, Sir Keith," the old man said.

"Why, Hamish, you seem to have lost all

your courage as soon as you put Colin Laing ashore."

"Colin Laing! Is it Colin Laing!" exclaimed Hamish, indignantly. "I will know how to sail this yacht, and I will know the banks, and the tides, and the rocks better than any fifteen thousands of Colin Laings!"

"And what if the *Dunara* is coming south? If she cannot see us, we can see her."

But whether it was that Colin Laing had before leaving the yacht managed to convey to Hamish some notion of the risk he was running, or whether it was that he was merely anxious for his master's safety, it was clear that Hamish was far from satisfied. He opened and shut his big clasp-knife in an awkward silence. Then he said—

"You will not go to Castle Dare, Sir Keith?"

Macleod started; he had forgotten that Hamish was there.

"No. I have told you where I am going."

"But there is not any good anchorage at that island, sir!" he protested. "Have I not been round every bay of it; and you too, Sir Keith; and you know there is not an inch of sand or of mud, but only the small loose stones. And then the shepherd they left there all by himself; it was mad he became at last, and took his own life too."

"Well, do you expect to see his ghost?" Macleod said. "Come, Hamish, you have lost your nerve in the south. Surely you are not afraid of being anywhere in the old yacht, so long as she has good sea-room around her?"

"And if you are not wishing to go up the Sound of Iona in the daylight, Sir Keith," Hamish said, still clinging to the point, "we could bear a little to the south, and go round the outside of Iona."

"The Dubh-artach men would recognise the *Umpire* at once," Macleod said, abruptly; and then he suggested to Hamish that he should get a little more way on the yacht, so that she might be a trifle steadier when Christina carried the dinner into the English lady's cabin. But indeed there was now little

breeze of any kind. Hamish's fears of a dead
calm were likely to prove true.

Meanwhile another conversation had been
going forward in the small cabin below,
that was now suffused by a beautiful warm light
reflected from the evening sky. Miss White
was looking very well now, after her long sea
voyage. During their first few hours in blue
water she had been very ill indeed; and she
repeatedly called on Christina to allow her
to die. The old Highlandwoman came to the
conclusion that English ladies were rather
childish in their ways; but the only answer
she made to this reiterated prayer was to make
Miss White as comfortable as was possible, and
to administer such restoratives as she thought
desirable. At length, when recovery and a
sound appetite set in, the patient began to
show a great friendship for Christina. There
. was no longer any theatrical warning of the
awful fate in store for everybody connected
with this enterprise. She tried rather to enlist
the old woman's sympathies on her behalf, and
if she did not very well succeed in that direc-

T 2

tion, at least she remained on friendly terms
with Christina, and received from her the
solace of much gossip about the whereabouts
and possible destination of the ship.

And on this evening Christina had an important piece of news.

"Where have we got to now, Christina?"
said Miss White, quite cheerfully, when the
old woman entered.

"Oh, yes, mem, we will still be off the
Mull shore, but a good piece away from it, and
there is not much wind, mem. But Hamish
thinks we will get to the anchorage the
night whateffer."

"The anchorage!" Miss White exclaimed
eagerly. "Where? You are going to Castle
Dare, surely?"

"No, mem, I think not," said Christina.
"I think it iss an island—but you will not
know the name of that island—there iss no
English for it at ahl."

"But where is it? Is it near Castle Dare?"

"Oh, no, mem; it iss a good way from
Castle Dare; and it iss out in the sea. Do

you know Gometra, mem ?—wass you ever going
out to Gometra ? "

" Yes, of course ; I remember something
about it anyway.",

" Ah, well, it is away out past Gometra,
mem ; and not a good place for an anchorage
whateffer ; but Hamish he will know ahl the
anchorages."

" What on earth is the use of going
there ? "

" I do not know, mem, if you please."

" Is Sir Keith going to keep me on board
this boat for ever ? "

" I do not know, mem."

Christina had to leave the cabin just then ;
when she returned she said, with some little
hesitation—

" If I wass mekking so bold, mem, ass to
say this to you : Why are you not asking
the questions of Sir Keith himself ? He will
know all about it ; and if you were to come
into the saloon, mem——"

" Do you think I would enter into any
communication with him after his treatment

of me ?" said Miss White, indignantly. "No ;
let him atone for that first. When he has
set me at liberty, then I will speak with him ;
but never so long as he keeps me shut up
like a convict."

"I wass only saying, mem," Christina
answered, with great respect, "that if you
were wishing to know where we were going, Sir
Keith will know that; but how can I know
it ? And you know, mem, Sir Keith has not
shut you up in this cabin : you hef the
saloon, if you would please to hef it."

"Thank you, I know !" rejoined Miss White.
"If I choose, my jail may consist of two rooms
instead of one. I don't appreciate that amount
of liberty. I want to be set ashore."

"That I hef nothing to do with, mem,"
Christina said ⎣humbly, proceeding with her
work.

Miss White, being left to think over these
things, was beginning to believe that, after all,
her obduracy was not likely to be of much
service to her. Would it not be wiser to treat
with the enemy : perhaps to outwit him by a

show of forgiveness? Here they were approaching the end of the voyage—at least, Christina seemed to intimate as much; and if they were not exactly within call of friends, they would surely be within rowing distance of some inhabited island, even Gometra, for example. And if only a message could be sent to Castle Dare? Lady Macleod and Janet Macleod were women. They would not countenance this monstrous thing. If she could only reach them, she would be safe.

The rose-pink died away from the long promontories, and was succeeded by a sombre grey; the glory in the west sank down; a wan twilight came over the sea and the sky; and a small golden star—like the point of a needle—told where the Dubh-artach men had lit their beacon for the coming night. The *Umpire* lay and idly rolled in this dead calm; Macleod paced up and down the deck, in the solemn stillness; Hamish threw a tarpaulin over the skylight of the saloon, to cover the bewildering light from below; and then, as the time went slowly by, darkness came over the land and the sea. They were alone with the night, and the lapping waves, and the stars.

About ten o'clock there was a loud rattling of blocks and cordage—the first puff of a coming breeze had struck her. The men were at their posts in a moment; there were a few sharp, quick orders from Hamish; and presently the old *Umpire*, with her great boom away over her quarter, was running free before a light south-easterly wind.

"Ay, ay!" said Hamish, in sudden gladness, "we will soon be by Ardalanish Point with a fine wind like this, Sir Keith; and if you would rather hef no lights on her—well, it is a clear night whateffer; and the *Dunara* she will hef up her lights."

The wind came in bits of squalls, it is true; but the sky overhead remained clear; and the *Umpire* bowled merrily along. Macleod was still on deck. They rounded the Ross of Mull; and got into the smoother waters of the Sound: would any of the people in the cottages at Erraidh see this grey ghost of a vessel go gliding past over the dark water? Behind them burned

the yellow eye of Dubh-artach; before them a few
small red points told them of the Iona cottages;
and still this phantom grey vessel held on her way.
The *Umpire* was nearing her last anchorage.

And still she steals onward, like a thief in the
night. She has passed through the Sound; she
is in the open sea again; there is a calling of
startled birds from over the dark bosom of the
deep. Then far away they watch the lights of a
steamer: but she is miles from their course; they
cannot even hear the throb of her engines.

It is another sound they hear—a low booming
as of distant thunder. And that black thing
away on their right—scarcely visible over the
darkened waves—is that the channelled and sea-
bird-haunted Staffa, trembling through all her
caves under the shock of the smooth Atlantic
surge? For despite the clearness of the starlit sky,
there is a wild booming of waters all around her
rocks; and the giant caverns answer; and the
thunder shudders out to the listening sea.

The night drags on. The Dutchman is fast
asleep in his vast Atlantic bed; the dull roar of
the waves he has heard for millions of years is

not likely to awake him. And Fladda, and Lunga: surely this ghost-grey ship that steals towards them is not the old *Umpire* that used to visit them in the gay summer-time, with her red ensign flying, and the blue seas all around her ? But here is a dark object on the waters that is growing larger and larger as one approaches it. The black outline of it is becoming sharp against the clear dome of stars. There is a gloom around as one gets nearer and nearer the bays and cliffs of this lonely island ; and now one hears the sound of breakers on the rocks. Hamish and his men are on the alert. The topsail has been lowered. The heavy chain of the anchor lies ready by the windlass. And then, as the *Umpire* glides into smooth water, and her head is brought round to the light breeze, away goes the anchor with a rattle that awakes a thousand echoes ; and all the startled birds among the rocks are calling through the night,—the sea-pyots screaming shrilly, the curlews uttering their warning note, the herons croaking as they wing their slow flight away across the sea. The *Umpire* has got to her anchorage at last.

And scarcely was the anchor down when they brought him a message from the English lady. She was in the saloon, and wished to see him. He could scarcely believe this; for it was now past midnight; and she had never come into the saloon before. But he went down through the forecastle; and through his own state-room; and opened the door of the saloon.

For a second the strong light almost blinded him; but at all events he knew she was sitting there; and that she was regarding him with no fierce indignation at all, but with quite a friendly look.

"Gertrude!" said he, in wonder; but he did not approach her. He stood before her as one who was submissive.

"So we have got to land at last," said she: and more and more he wondered to hear the friendliness of her voice. Could it be true, then? Or was it only one of those visions that had of late been torturing his brain?

"Oh, yes, Gerty!" said he. "We have got to an anchorage."

"I thought I would sit up for it," said she.

" Christina said we should get to land some time
to-night ; and I thought I would like to see you.
Because you know, Keith, you have used me
very badly.   And won't you sit down ? "

He accepted that invitation.   *Could it be
true? could it be true?*   This was ringing in
his ears.   He heard her only in a bewildered
way.

"And I want you to tell me what you mean to
do with me," said she, frankly and graciously ;
" I am at your mercy, Keith."

"Oh, not that—not that," said he ; and he
added, sadly enough, " it is I who have been at
your mercy since ever I saw you, Gerty ; and it
is for you to say what is to become of you and
of me.   And have you got over your anger now ?
—and will you think of all that made me do
this, and try to forgive it for the sake of my love
for you, Gerty ?   Is there any chance of that
now ? "

She rather avoided the earnest gaze that was
bent on her.   She did not notice how nervously
his hand gripped the edge of the table near him.

" Well, it is a good deal to forgive, Keith ;

you will acknowledge that yourself; and though you used to think that I was ready to sacrifice everything for fame, I did not expect you would make me a nine-days' wonder in this way. I suppose the whole thing is in the papers now ?"

"Oh, no, Gerty; I sent a message to your father."

"Well, that was kind of you. And audacious. Were you not afraid of his overtaking you ? The *Umpire* is not the swiftest of sailers, you used to say ; and you know there are telegraphs and railways to all the ports."

"He did not know you were in the *Umpire*, Gerty. But of course, if he were very anxious about you, he would write or come to Dare. I should not be surprised if he were there now."

A quick look of surprise and gladness sprang to her face

"Papa—at Castle Dare !" she exclaimed. "And Christina says it is not far from here."

"Not many miles away."

"Then, of course, they will know we are here in the morning !" she cried, in the indiscretion of sudden joy. "And they will come out for me."

"Oh no, Gerty, they will not come out for you. No human being but those on board knows that we are here. Do you think they could see you from Dare? And there is no one living now on the island. We are alone in the sea."

The light died away from her face; but she said, cheerfully enough—

"Well, I am at your mercy then, Keith. Let us take it that way. Now you must tell me what part in the comedy you mean me to play; for the life of me I can't make it out."

"Oh, Gerty, Gerty, do not speak like that!" he exclaimed. "You are breaking my heart. Is there none of the old love left? Is it all a matter for jesting?"

She saw she had been incautious.

"Well," said she, gently, "I was wrong; I know it is more serious than that; and I am not indisposed to forgive you, if you treat me fairly. I know you have great earnestness of nature; and—and you were very fond of me; and although you have risked a great deal in what you have done, still, men who are very deeply in love don't think much about consequences. And if I were to forgive you, and make friends again, what then ? "

" And if we were as we used to be," said he, with a grave wistfulness in his face, " do you not think I would gladly take you ashore, Gerty ? "

" And to Castle Dare ? "

" Oh, yes, to Castle Dare ! Would not my mother and Janet be glad to welcome you ! "

" And papa may be there ? "

" If he is not there, can we not telegraph for him ? Why, Gerty, surely you would not be married anywhere but in the Highlands ? "

At the mention of marriage she blanched somewhat ; but she had nerved herself to play this part.

" Then, Keith," said she, gallantly, " I will make you a promise. Take me to Castle Dare to-morrow, and the moment I am within its doors, I will shake hands with you, and forgive you, and we will be friends again as in the old days."

" We were more than friends, Gerty," said he, in a low voice.

" Let us be friends first, and then who knows

what may not follow ?" said she, brightly. "You
cannot expect me to be over-profuse in affection
just after being shut up like this ?"

"Gerty," said he, and he looked at her with
those strangely tired eyes, and there was a great
gentleness in his voice, " do you know where you
are ? You are close to the island that I told
you of—where I wish to have my grave on the
cliff. But instead of a grave, would it not be a
fine thing to have a marriage here ? No, do not
be alarmed, Gerty ! it is only with your own
good will ; and surely your heart will consent at
last ! Would not that be a strange wedding,
too ; with the minister from Salen ; and your
father on board ; and the people from Dare ? Oh,
you would see such a number of boats come out
that day, and we would go proudly back ; and
do you not think there would be a great re-
joicing that day ? Then all our troubles would
be at an end, Gerty ! There would be no more
fear ; and the theatres would never see you
again ; and the long, happy life we should
lead, we two together ! And do you know the
first thing I would get you, Gerty ?—it would be

a new yacht! I would go to the Clyde, and have it built all for you. I would not have you go out again in this yacht, for you would then remember the days in which I was cruel to you ; but in a new yacht you would not remember that any more ; and do you not think we would have many a pleasant, long summer day on the deck of her, and only ourselves, Gerty ! And you would sing the songs I first heard you sing, and I think the sailors would imagine they heard the singing of the mermaid of Colonsay, for there is no one can sing as you can sing, Gerty. I think it was that first took away my heart from me."

"But we can talk about all these things when I am on shore again," said she, coldly. "You cannot expect me to be very favourably disposed so long as I am shut up here."

"But then," he said, "if you were on shore you might go away again from me, Gerty ! The people would get at your ear again ; they would whisper things to you ; you would think about the theatres again. I have saved you, sweetheart ; can I let you go back ? "

The words were spoken with an eager affection and yearning ; but they sank into her mind with a dull and cold conviction that there was no escape for her through any way of artifice.

"Am I to understand, then ?" said she, "that you mean to keep me a prisoner here until I marry you ?"

"Why do you speak like that, Gerty ?"

"I demand an answer to my question."

"I have risked everything to save you; can I let you go back ?"

A sudden flash of desperate anger—even of hatred—was in her eyes ; her fine piece of acting had been of no avail.

"Well, let the farce end !" said she, with frowning eyebrows. "Before I came on board this yacht I had some pity for you. I thought you were at least a man, and had a man's generosity. Now I find you a coward, and a tyrant——"

"Gerty !"

"Oh, do not think you have frightened me with your stories of the revenge of your miserable chiefs, and their savage slaves ! Not a bit of it! Do with me what you like; I would not marry you if you gave me a hundred yachts!"

"Gerty!"

The anguish of his face was growing wild with despair.

"I say, let the farce end! I had pity for you—yes I had! Now—I hate you!"

He sprang up with a quick cry, as of one shot through the heart. He regarded her, in a bewildered manner, for one brief second; and then he gently said, "Good-night, Gerty! God forgive you!" and he staggered backwards, and got out of the saloon, leaving her alone.

See! the night is still fine. All around this solitary bay there is a wall of rock, jet black, against the clear, dark sky, with its myriad twinkling stars. The new moon has arisen; but it sheds but little radiance yet down there in the south. There is a sharper gleam from one lambent planet—a thin line of golden-yellow light that comes all the way across from the black rocks until it breaks in flashes among the ripples close to the side of the yacht. Silence once more reigns around; only from time to time one hears the croak of a heron from the dusky shore.

What can keep this man up so late on deck? There is nothing to look at but the great bows of the yacht black against the pale grey sea; and the tall spars and the rigging going away up into the starlit sky; and the suffused glow from the skylight touching a yellow-grey on the boom. There is no need for the anchor-watch that Hamish has been talking about. The equinoctials are not likely to begin on such a calm night as this.

He is looking across the lapping grey water to the jet black line of cliff. And there are certain words haunting him. He cannot forget them. He cannot put them away.

*   *   *   *

WHEREFORE IS LIGHT GIVEN TO HIM THAT IS IN MISERY, AND LIFE UNTO THE BITTER IN SOUL? *   *   * WHICH LONG FOR DEATH, BUT IT COMETH NOT; AND DIG FOR IT MORE THAN FOR HIDDEN TREASURES. *   *   * WHICH REJOICE

EXCEEDINGLY, AND ARE GLAD WHEN THEY CAN
FIND THE GRAVE.

*   *   *   *

Then in the stillness of the night, he heard a
breathing. He went forward; and found that
Hamish had secreted himself behind the windlass. He uttered some exclamation in the Gaelic;
and the old man rose and stood guiltily before him.

"Have I not told you to go below before;
and will I have to throw you down into the
forecastle?"

The old man stood irresolute for a moment.
Then he said, also in his native tongue:

"You should not speak like that to me, Sir
Keith: I have known you many a year."

Macleod caught Hamish's hand.

"I beg your pardon, Hamish. You do not
know. It is a sore heart I have this night."

"Oh, God help us! Do I not know that!"
he exclaimed, in a broken voice; and Macleod,
as he turned away, could hear the old man crying
bitterly in the dark. What else could Hamish
do now—for him who had been to him as the
son of his old age?

"Go below now, Hamish," said Macleod in a gentle voice; and the old man slowly and reluctantly obeyed.

But the night had not drawn to day when Macleod again went forward and said, in a strange, excited whisper—

"Hamish, Hamish, are you awake now?"

Instantly the old man appeared : he had not turned into his berth at all.

"Hamish, Hamish, do you hear the sound?" Macleod said, in the same wild way, "do you not hear the sound?"

"What sound, Sir Keith?" said he—for indeed there was nothing but the lapping of the water along the side of the yacht and a murmur of ripples along the shore.

"Do you not hear it, Hamish? It is a sound as of a brass band!—a brass band playing music —as if it was in a theatre. Can you not hear it, Hamish?"

"Oh, God help us! God help us!" Hamish cried.

"You do not hear it, Hamish?" he said. "Ah, it is some mistake. I beg your pardon for calling you, Hamish : now you will go below again."

"Oh, no, Sir Keith," said Hamish. "Will I not stay on deck now till the morning? It is a fine sleep I have had. Oh, yes, I had a fine sleep. And how is one to know when the equinoctials may not come on?"

"I wish you to go below, Hamish."

And now this sound that is ringing in his ears is no longer of the brass band that he had heard in the theatre. It is quite different. It has all the ghastly mirth of the song that Norman Ogilvie used to sing in the old, half-forgotten days. What is it that he hears?

＊　　　＊　　　＊　　　＊

King Death was a rare old fellow,
He sate where no sun could shine ;
And he lifted his hand so yellow,
And poured out his coal-black wine !
Hurrah ! hurrah ! hurrah ! for the coal-black wine !

It is a strange mirth. It might almost make a man laugh. For do we not laugh gently when we bury a young child, and put the flowers over it ; and know that it is at peace? The child has no more pain at the heart. Oh, Norman Ogilvie, are you still singing the wild song; and are you laughing now?—or is it the old man Hamish that is crying in the dark?

    *   *

> *There came to him many a maiden,*
> *Whose eyes had forgot to shine;*
> *And widows with grief o'erladen,*
> *For a draught of his sleepy wine.*
> *Hurrah! hurrah! hurrah! for the coal-black wine!*

It is such a fine thing to sleep—when one has been fretting all the night, and spasms of fire go through the brain! Ogilvie, Ogilvie, do you remember the laughing Duchess: do you think she would laugh over one's grave? Or put her foot on it, and stand relentless, with anger in her eyes? That is a sad thing; but after it is over there is sleep.

  *   *   *   *

> *All came to the rare old fellow*
> *Who laughed till his eyes dropped brine,*
> *As he gave them his hand so yellow,*
> *And pledged them, in Death's black wine!*
> *Hurrah! hurrah! hurrah! for the coal-black wine!*

Hamish!—Hamish!—will you not keep her away from me? I have told Donald what pibroch he will play; I want to be at peace now. But the brass band—the brass band—I can hear the blare of the trumpets; and Ulva will know that we are here, and the Gometra men, and the sea-birds too, that I used to love. But she has killed all that now, and she stands on my grave. She will laugh; for she was light-hearted; like a young child. But you, Hamish, you will find the quiet grave for me; and Donald will play the pibroch for me that I told him of; and you will say no word to her of all that is over and gone.

* * * * *

See — he sleeps. This haggard-faced man is stretched on the deck; and the pale dawn, arising in the east, looks at him; and does not revive him, but makes him whiter still. You might almost think he was dead. But Hamish knows better than that; for the old man comes stealthily forward; and he has a great tartan plaid in his hands; and very gently indeed he puts it over his young master. And there are tears running down Hamish's face; and he says, "The brave lad! The brave lad!"

CHAPTER XV.

"DUNCAN," said Hamish, in a low whisper—for Macleod had gone below, and they thought he might be asleep in the small, hushed state-room— "this is a strange-looking day, is it not? And I am afraid of it in this open bay, with an anchorage no better than a sheet of paper for an anchorage. Do you see now, how strange-looking it is?"

Duncan Cameron also spoke in his native tongue; and he said—

"That is true, Hamish. And it was a day like this there was when the *Solan* was sunk at her moorings in Loch Hourn. Do you remember, Hamish? And it would be better for us now if we were in Loch Tua, or Loch na Keal, or in the dock that was built for the steamer at Tiree. I do not like the look of this day."

Yet to an ordinary observer it would have seemed that the chief characteristic of this pale, still day was extreme and settled calm. There was not a breath of wind to ruffle the surface of the sea; but there was a slight, glassy swell; and that only served to show curious opalescent tints under the suffused light of the sun. There were no clouds; there was only a thin veil of faint and sultry mist all across the sky; the sun was invisible, but there was a glare of yellow at one point of the heavens. A dead calm; but heavy, oppressed, sultry. There was something in the atmosphere that seemed to weigh on the chest.

"There was a dream I had this morning," continued Hamish, in the same low tones. "It was about my little granddaughter Christina. You know my little Christina, Duncan. And she said to me: 'What have you done with Sir Keith Macleod? Why have you not brought him back? He was under your care, grandfather.' I did not like that dream."

"Oh, you are becoming as bad as Sir Keith
Macleod himself!" said the other. "He does
not sleep. He talks to himself. You will become like that if you pay attention to foolish
dreams, Hamish."

Hamish's quick temper leapt up.

"What do you mean, Duncan Cameron, by
saying 'as bad as Sir Keith Macleod'? You
—you come from Ross: perhaps they have not
good masters there. I tell you there is not any
man in Ross, or in Sutherland either, is as
good a master, and as brave a lad, as Sir Keith
Macleod—not any one, Duncan Cameron!"

"I did not mean anything like that, Hamish,"
said the other humbly. "But there was a breeze
this morning. We could have got over to Loch
Tua. Why did we stay here, where there is no
shelter, and no anchorage? Do you know what
is likely to come after a day like this?"

"It is your business to be a sailor on board
this yacht; it is not your business to say where
she will go," said Hamish.

But all the same the old man was becoming
more and more alarmed at the ugly aspect of

this dead calm. The very birds, instead of stalking among the still pools, or lying buoyant on the smooth waters, were excitedly calling, and whirring from one point to another.

"If the equinoctials were to begin now," said Duncan Cameron, "this is a fine place to meet the equinoctials! An open bay, without shelter; and a ground that is no ground for an anchorage. It is not two anchors or twenty anchors would hold in such a ground; and there are rocks all round us that would put the *Clansman* herself to pieces in a moment."

Macleod appeared: the men were suddenly silent. Without a word to either of them—and that was not his wont—he passed to the stern of the yacht. Hamish knew from his manner that he would not be spoken to. He did not follow him, even with all this vague dread on his mind.

The day wore on to the afternoon. Macleod, who had been pacing up and down the deck, suddenly called Hamish. Hamish came aft at once.

"Hamish," said he, with a strange sort of laugh, "do you remember this morning, before

the light came? Do you remember that I asked
you about a brass band that I heard playing?"

Hamish looked at him; and said with an
earnest anxiety—

"Oh, Sir Keith, you will pay no heed to that!
It is very common. I have heard them say it
is very common. Why, to hear a brass band,
to be sure! There is nothing more common
than that. And you will not think you are
unwell merely because you think you can hear
a brass band playing!"

"I want you to tell me, Hamish," said he,
in the same jesting way, "whether my eyes
have followed the example of my ears, and are
playing tricks. Do you think they are blood-
shot, with my lying on deck in the cold?
Hamish, what do you see all around?"

The old man looked at the sky, and the shore,
and the sea. It was a marvellous thing. The
world was all enshrouded in a salmon-coloured
mist: there was no line of horizon visible
between the sea and the sky.

"It is red, Sir Keith," said Hamish.

'Ah! Am I in my senses this time? And

what do you think of a red day, Hamish?
That is not a usual thing."

"Oh, Sir Keith, it will be a wild night this
night! And we cannot stay here, with this bad
anchorage!"

"And where would you go, Hamish—in a
dead calm?" Macleod asked, still with a smile
on the wan face.

"Where would I go?" said the old man,
excitedly. "I—I will take care of the yacht.
But you, Sir Keith; oh! you—you will go
ashore now. Do you know, sir, the sheiling
that the shepherd had? It is a poor place;
oh, yes; but Duncan Cameron and I will take
some things ashore. And do you not think we
can look after the yacht? She has met the
equinoctials before, if it is the equinoctials that
are beginning. She has met them before; and
cannot she meet them now? But you, Sir
Keith, you will go ashore!"

Macleod burst out laughing, in an odd sort
of way.

"Do you think I am good at running away
when there is any kind of danger, Hamish?

Have you got into the English belief? Would
you call me a coward, too? Nonsense, nonsense, nonsense, Hamish!—I—why, I am going
to drink a glass of the coal-black wine, and
have done with it. I will drink it to the health
of my sweetheart, Hamish!"

"Sir Keith," said the old man, beginning to
tremble, though he but half understood the
meaning of this scornful mirth, "I have had
charge of you since you were a young lad."

"Very well!"

"And Lady Macleod will ask of me, 'Such
and such a thing happened: what did you do
for my son?' Then I will say, 'Your ladyship,
we were afraid of the equinoctials; and we got
Sir Keith to go ashore; and when the gale was
over we went ashore for him; and now we have
brought him back to Castle Dare!'"

"Hamish, Hamish, you are laughing at me!
Or you want to call me a coward? Don't you
know I should be afraid of the ghost of the
shepherd who killed himself? Don't you know
that the English people call me a coward?"

"May their souls dwell in the downmost hall

of perdition!" said Hamish, with his cheeks become a grey-white; "and every woman that ever came of the accursed race!"

Macleod looked at the old man for a second; and he gripped his hand.

"Do not say that, Hamish—that is folly. But you have been my friend. My mother will not forget you—it is not the way of a Macleod to forget—whatever happens to me."

"Sir Keith!" Hamish cried, "I do not know what you mean. But you will go ashore before the night!"

"Go ashore?" Macleod answered, with a return to the wild, bantering tone, "when I am going to see my sweetheart? Oh, no! Tell Christina, now! Tell Christina to ask the young English lady to come into the saloon, for I have something to say to her. Be quick, Hamish!"

Hamish went away; and before long he returned with the answer that the young English lady was in the saloon. And now he was no longer haggard and piteous; but joyful; and there was a strange light in his eyes.

"Sweetheart," said he, "are you waiting for

me at last? I have brought you a long way.
Shall we drink a glass together now at the end
of the voyage?"

"Do you wish to insult me?" said she;
but there was no anger in her voice: there was
more of fear in her eyes, as she regarded him.

"You have no other message for me than
the one you gave me last night, Gerty?" said
he, almost cheerfully. "It is all over then?
You would go away from me for ever? But
we will drink a glass before we go!"

He sprang forward, and caught both her
hands in his with the grip of a vice.

"Do you know what you have done, Gerty?"
said he, in a low voice. "Oh, you have soft,
smooth, English ways; and you are like a rose-
leaf; and you are like a queen, whom all people
are glad to serve. But do you know that
you have killed a man's life? There is no
penalty for that in the south, perhaps; but
you are no longer in the south. And if you
have this very night to drink a glass with me,
you will not refuse it? It is only a glass of
the coal-black wine!"

She struggled back from him; for there was a look in his face that frightened her. But she had a wonderful self-command.

"Is that the message I was to hear?" said she, coldly.

"Why, sweetheart, are you not glad? Is not that the only gladness left for you and for me, that we should drink one glass together, and clasp hands, and say good-bye? What else is there left? What else could come to you and to me? And it may not be this night, or to-morrow night; but one night soon I think it will come; and then, sweetheart, we will have one more glass together, before the end!"

He went on deck. He called Hamish.

"Hamish," said he, in a grave, matter-of-fact way, "I don't like the look of this evening. Did you say the sheiling was still on the island?"

"Oh, yes, Sir Keith," said Hamish, with great joy, for he thought his advice was about to be taken after all.

"Well, now, you know the gales, when they begin, sometimes last for two, or three, or four days; and I will ask you to see that Christina takes a good store of things to the sheiling, before the darkness comes on. Take plenty of things now, Hamish, and put them in the sheiling, for I am afraid this is going to be a wild night."

All the red light had gone away; and as the sun went down, there was nothing but a spectral whiteness over the sea and the sky. And the atmosphere was so close and sultry that it seemed to suffocate one. Moreover, there was a dead calm; if they had wanted to get away from this exposed place, how could they? They could not get into the gig and pull this great yacht over to Loch-na-Keal.

It was with a light heart that Hamish set about this thing; and Christina forthwith filled a hamper with tinned meats, and bread, and whisky, and what not. And fuel was taken ashore, too; and candles, and a store of matches. If the gales were coming on, as appeared likely from this ominous-looking evening, who could tell how many days and nights the young master—and the English lady, too, if he

desired her company—might not have to stay
ashore, while the men took the chance of the sea
with the yacht, or perhaps seized the occasion
of a lull to make for some place of shelter?'
There was Loch Tua; and there was the bay at
Bunessan; and there was the little channel called
Polterriv, behind the rocks opposite Iona. Any
shelter at all was better than this exposed place,
with the treacherous anchorage.

Hamish and Duncan Cameron returned to the
yacht.

"Will you go ashore now, Sir Keith," the old
man said.

"Oh, no; I am not going ashore yet. It is
not yet time to run away, Hamish."

He spoke in a friendly and pleasant fashion,
though Hamish, in his increasing alarm, thought
it no proper time for jesting. They hauled the
gig up to the davits, however, and again the
yacht lay in dead silence in this little bay.

The evening grew to dusk; the only change
visible in the spectral world of pale yellow-
white mist was the appearance in the sky of a
number of small, detached, bulbous-looking

clouds of a dusky blue-grey. They had not drifted hither, for there was no wind. They had only appeared. They were absolutely motionless.

But the heat and the suffocation in this atmosphere became almost insupportable. The men, with bare heads, and jerseys unbuttoned at the neck, were continually going to the cask of fresh water beside the windlass. Nor was there any change when the night came on. If anything, the night was hotter than the evening had been. They awaited in silence what might come of this ominous calm.

Hamish came aft.

"I beg your pardon, Sir Keith," said he, "but I have put up the side-lights, in case there is a chance of our getting away; and I am thinking we will have an anchor-watch to-night."

"You will have no anchor-watch to-night," Macleod answered slowly, from out of the darkness. "I will be all the anchor-watch you will need, Hamish, until the morning."

"You, sir!" Hamish cried. "I have been waiting to take you ashore! and surely it is ashore that you are going!"

Just as he had spoken there was a sudden sound that all the world seemed to stand still to hear. It was a low, murmuring sound of thunder; but it was so remote as almost to be inaudible. The next moment an awful thing occurred. The two men standing face to face in the dark suddenly found themselves in a blaze of blinding steel-blue light; and at the very same instant the thunder-roar crackled and shook all around them like the firing of a thousand cannon. How the wild echoes went booming over the sea! Then they were in the black night again. There was a period of awed silence.

"Hamish," Macleod said, quickly, "do as I tell you now! Lower the gig; take the men with you, and Christina; and go ashore and remain in the sheiling till the morning."

"I will not!" Hamish cried. "Oh, Sir Keith, would you have me do that!"

Macleod had anticipated his refusal. Instantly he went forward and called up Christina. He ordered Duncan Cameron and John Cameron to lower away the gig. He got them all in but Hamish.

"Hamish," said he, "you are a smaller man than I. Is it on such a night that you would have me quarrel with you? Must I throw you into the boat?"

The old man clasped his trembling hands together as if in prayer; and he said, with an agonised and broken voice—

"Oh, Sir Keith, you are my master, and there is nothing I will not do for you; but only this one night you will let me remain with the yacht. I will give you the rest of my life; but only this one night——"

"Into the gig with you!" Macleod cried, angrily. "Why, man, don't you think I can keep anchor-watch?" But then he added, very gently, "Hamish, shake hands with me now. You were my friend; and you must get ashore before the sea rises."

"I will stay in the dingay, then;" the old man entreated.

"You will go ashore, Hamish; and this very instant, too. If the gale begins, how will you get ashore? Good-bye, Hamish—*good-night.*"

Another blue-white sheet of flame quivered

all around them, just as this black figure was
descending into the gig; and then the fierce
hell of sounds broke loose once more. Land
and sky together seemed to shudder at the
wild uproar; and far away the sounds went
thundering through the hollow night. How
could one hear if there was any sobbing in
that departing boat—or any last cry of farewell?
It was Ulva calling now; and Fladda answering
from over the black water; and the Dutchman
is surely awake at last!

There came a stirring of wind—from the east,
and the sea began to moan. Surely the poor
fugitives must have reached the shore now?
And then there was a new and strange noise in
the distance; in the awful silence between the
peals of thunder it could be heard; it came
nearer and nearer — a low murmuring noise,
but full of a secret life and thrill—it came
along like the tread of a thousand armies—
and then the gale struck its first blow! The
yacht reeled under the stroke; then her bows
staggered up again like a dog that has been
felled; and after one or two convulsive

plunges, she clung hard at the strained cables.
And now the gale was growing in fury, and
the sea rising. Blinding showers of rain
swept over, hissing and roaring; the blue-white
tongues of flame were shooting this way and
that across the startled heavens; and there was
a more awful thunder than even the roar of
the Atlantic booming into the great sea-
caves. In the abysmal darkness the spectral
arms of the ocean rose white in their angry
clamour; and then another blue gleam would
lay bare the great heaving and writhing bosom
of the deep. What devil's dance is this?
Surely it cannot be Ulva—Ulva the green-
shored—Ulva that the sailors in their love of
her call softly *Ool-a-va*—that is laughing aloud
with wild laughter on this fearful night? And
Colonsay, and Lunga, and Fladda—they were
beautiful and quiet in the still summer-time;
but now they have gone mad; and they are
flinging back the plunging sea in white masses
of foam; and they are shrieking in their fierce
joy of the strife. And Staffa — Staffa is far
away and alone; she is trembling to her core;

NEARING THE END.   *To face p. 314, vol. iii.*

how long will the shuddering caves withstand the mighty hammer of the Atlantic surge? And then again the sudden wild gleam startles the night — and one sees, with an appalling vividness, the driven white waves and the black islands — and then again a thousand echoes go booming along the iron-bound coast. What can be heard in the roar of the hurricane, and the hissing of rain, and the thundering whirl of the waves on the rocks? surely not the one glad last cry: SWEETHEART! YOUR HEALTH! YOUR HEALTH IN THE COAL-BLACK WINE!

The poor fugitives crouching in among the rocks: is it the blinding rain or the driven white surf that is in their eyes? But they have sailor's eyes; they can see through the awful storm; and their gaze is fixed on one small green point far out there in the blackness—the starboard light of the doomed ship. It wavers like a will-o'-the-wisp; but it does not recede; the old *Umpire* still clings bravely to her anchor cables.

And amid all the din of the storm they hear

the voice of Hamish lifted aloud in lamentation :

"Oh, the brave lad ! The brave lad ! And
who is to save my young master now ; and who
will carry this tale back to Castle Dare ? They
will say to me ; 'Hamish, you had charge of
the young lad ; you put the first gun in his
hand ; you had charge of him ; he had the love
of a son for you : what is it you have done with
him this night ?' He is my Absalom ; he is my
brave young lad : oh, do you think that I will
let him drown and do nothing to try to save
him ? Do you think that ? Duncan Cameron :
are you a man ? Will you get into the gig
with me and pull out to the *Umpire ?* "

"By God," said Duncan Cameron, solemnly,
"I will do that. I have no wife ; I do not
care. I will go into the gig with you, Hamish;
but we will never reach the yacht—this night
or any night that is to come."

Then the old woman Christina shrieked aloud ;
and caught her husband by the arm.

"Hamish ! Hamish ! Are you going to drown
yourself before my eyes ? "

He shook her hand away from him.

"My young master ordered me ashore: I have come ashore. But I myself I order myself back again: Duncan Cameron, they will never say that we stood by and saw Macleod of Dare go down to his grave!"

They emerged from the shelter of this great rock—the hurricane was so fierce that they had to cling to one boulder after another to save themselves from being whirled into the sea. But were these two men by themselves? Not likely! It was the whole of the crew, five men in all, who now clambered along the slippery rocks to the shingle up which they had hauled the gig; and one wild lightning-flash saw them with their hands on the gunwale, ready to drag her down to the water. There was a surf raging there that would have swamped twenty gigs: these five men were going of their own free will and choice to certain death— so much had they loved the young master.

But a piercing cry from Christina arrested them. They looked out to sea. What was this sudden and awful thing?—instead of the star-

board green light, behold! the port red light
—and that moving! Oh, see! how it recedes,
wavering—flickering through the whirling vapour
of the storm! Is it a witch's dance; or are they
strange death-fires hovering over the dark ocean-
grave? But Hamish knows too well what it
means; and with a wild cry of horror and
despair, the old man sinks on his knees, and
clasps his hands, and stretches them out to
the terrible sea.

"Oh, Macleod, Macleod, are you going away
from me for ever? and we will go up the hills
together and on the lochs together no more—
no more—no more! Oh, the brave lad that
he was!—and the good master!—and who was
not proud of him?—my handsome lad!—and
he the last of the Macleods of Dare!"

*　　　*　　　*　　　*

Arise, Hamish, and have the gig hauled up
into shelter; for will you not want it when the
gale abates, and the seas are smooth, and you
have to go away to Dare, you and your com-
rades, with silent tongues and sombre eyes?

Why this wild lamentation in the darkness of the night? The stricken heart that you loved so well has found peace at last; the coal-black wine has been drunk; there is an end. And you, you poor, cowering fugitives, who only see each other's terrified faces when the wan gleam of the lightning blazes through the sky, perhaps it is well that you should weep and wail for the young master; but that is soon over; and the fierce white day will break. And this is what I am thinking of now: when the hurricane is gone, and the seas are smooth once more, then which of you—oh, which of you all will tell this tale to the two women at Castle Dare?

So fair shines the morning sun on the white sands of Iona! The three-days' gale is over; behold! how Ulva—Ulva the green-shored—the *Ool-a-va* that the sailors love—is laughing out again to the clear skies. And the great skarts on the shores of Erisgeir are spreading abroad their dusky wings to get them dried in the sun; and the seals are basking on the rocks in

Loch-na-Keal; and in Loch Scridain the white
gulls sit buoyant on the blue sea. There go
the Gometra men in their brown-sailed boat
to look after the lobster-traps at Staffa; and
very soon you will see the steamer come round
the far Cailleach Point; over at Erraidh they
are signalling to the men at Dubh-artach; and
they are glad to have a message from them after
the heavy gale. The new, bright day has begun;
the world has awakened again to the joyous
sunlight; there is a chattering of the sea-birds
all along the shores. It is a bright, eager, glad
day for all the world. But there is silence in
Castle Dare.

THE END.

LONDON: R. CLAY, SONS, AND TAYLOR, PRINTERS.

NOVELS

BY

WILLIAM BLACK.

THE STRANGE ADVENTURES OF A PHAETON.

ELEVENTH THOUSAND. Crown 8vo, 6s.

" Also, I have had it long on my mind to name 'The Adventures of a Phaeton' as a very delightful and wise book of its kind; very full of pleasant play, and deep and pure feeling; much interpretation of some of the best points of German character; and, last and least, with pieces of description in it which I should be glad, selfishly, to think inferior to what the public praise in 'Modern Painters,'— I can only say they seem to me quite as good."—*Mr. Ruskin in " Fors Clavigera,"* *March,* 1878.

A PRINCESS OF THULE.

TWELFTH THOUSAND. Crown 8vo, 6s.

"Pour goûter dans tout ce qu'elle a d'exquis l'histoire des amours dù peintre de Londres et de la fille des Hébrides, il faut la lire au grand air; c'est un roman d'été, et l'illusion est plus complète si l'on y peut ajouter le bruit du vent à travers les feuilles et les parfums d'une forêt ou d'un champ. Une autre condition, c'est de ne point être pressé. M. William Black ne l'est jamais. Il ne se lasse pas de promener son lecteur dans le monde inconnu qu'il a découvert, et l'on n'éprouve aucune envie de s'en plaindre, tant ces descriptions ont de charme, tant sont originales dans leur simplicité les figures qu'on y rencontre."—*" Un Romancier Ecossais,"* *Revue des Deux Mondes, October* 1, 1877.

MADCAP VIOLET.

EIGHTH THOUSAND. Crown 8vo, 6s.

" We take it that an indefinable confusion of moods, a swift transition from the humorous to the pathetic, is one of the signs of real literary genius, and assuredly it is very conspicuous in Mr. Black. No one shows more sympathetic delight in the brightest scenes of life and nature. No one revels more heartily in the delineation of a joyous character, or in the description of beautiful and be- witching scenery; but the broad under-vein of melancholy will crop out from time to time, and when he is being wrought up towards the most brilliant inspira- tion in his stories, he almost invariably inclines to become sad and sombre. . . . . . . And now 'Madcap Violet,' with her wild spirits and irrepressible inde- pendence, is made to point the moral of the vicissitudes of life, while her buoyancy is extinguished in unmitigated tragedy. We are inclined to cling to the good old tradition of the final triumph of love and virtue in the shape of brightening fortunes and a happy marriage. But if ingeniously-wrought sympathy and the ex- citement of an intense emotional interest are the tests of a powerful and success- ful novel, we place Mr. Black's 'Madcap Violet' in a very high rank indeed."— *Times.*

GREEN PASTURES AND PICCADILLY.

Cheaper Edition. Crown 8vo, 6s.

THE MAID OF KILLEENA, and other

TALES. New Edition. Crown 8vo, 6s.

MACMILLAN & CO., LONDON.

www.ingramcontent.com/pod-product-compliance
Lightning Source LLC
Chambersburg PA
CBHW031338070726
47496CB00017B/1219